S0-BTQ-321

With Murder in Mind
LP BREAM

21280

39204000025311

Bream, Freda
Gilpin County Public Library
Gilpin County Public Library

SPECIAL MESSAGE TO READERS

This book is published by

THE ULVERSCROFT FOUNDATION,

a registered charity in the U.K., No. 264873

The Foundation was established in 1974 to provide funds to help towards research, diagnosis and treatment of eye diseases. Below are a few examples of contributions made by THE ULVERSCROFT FOUNDATION:

★ A new Children's Assessment Unit at Moorfield's Hospital, London.

★ Twin operating theatres at the Western Ophthalmic Hospital, London.

★ The Frederick Thorpe Ulverscroft Chair of Ophthalmology at the University of Leicester.

★ Eye Laser equipment to various eye hospitals.

If you would like to help further the work of the Foundation by making a donation or leaving a legacy, every contribution, no matter how small, is received with gratitude. Please write for details to:

THE ULVERSCROFT FOUNDATION,
The Green, Bradgate Road, Anstey,
Leicestershire, LE7 7FU. England.
Telephone: (0533) 364325

WITH MURDER IN MIND

The advertisement read: "A New Zealand family wish to employ a well-spoken young English woman as companion to two children." Pamela was delighted when she landed the job but life in New Zealand did not turn out as she expected. The sun shone, the family were friendly, and her duties were light, but unexplained accidents began to happen. Had she been lured to the other side of the world simply to be murdered? But why should anyone wish to harm her? When she consulted the local vicar, Jabal Jarrett, he took the matter seriously and advised her to fly straight back home. She was soon to wish she had taken his advice.

Books by Freda Bream
in the Linford Mystery Library:

ISLAND OF FEAR
THE VICAR INVESTIGATES
WITH MURDER IN MIND

LP
BREAM

FREDA BREAM

WITH MURDER IN MIND

Complete and Unabridged

LINFORD
Leicester

First Linford Edition
published May 1990

Copyright © 1985 by Freda Bream
All rights reserved

British Library CIP Data

Bream, Freda
With murder in mind.—Large print ed.—
Linford mystery library
I. Title
823'.914[F]

ISBN 0-7089-6892-9

Published by
F. A. Thorpe (Publishing) Ltd.
Anstey, Leicestershire

Set by Rowland Phototypesetting Ltd.
Bury St. Edmunds, Suffolk
Printed and bound in Great Britain by
T. J. Press (Padstow) Ltd., Padstow, Cornwall

1

I'M alive. I'm still alive. I may not be in an hour's time, but then neither may you. A mason could drop a brick on your head or a drunken driver run you down. A power cable may fall across your front path and frizzle you to a molten blob before you have time to be aware that you've stepped on it. At least I *know* my danger. I know the form it will take and from where it will come.

I'm frightened. All right, I admit it. It comes on me in waves, a sort of cold shiver, starting at my ankles and trembling upwards through all my muscles until it wraps me in a chilly shroud. Then it passes and I start hoping again. Like hoping the vicar will get here in time.

It all began with this ad. in the *Daily Telegraph*. No, it didn't. It began with finding out about Talbot, the man I intended to marry. I'd been really taken in by that guy. He was tall, dark and good-looking, with one of those intriguing faces that give promise of exciting unknown qualities. But you can't tell. Mr. Jarrett says you can read emotions from someone's features but seldom character and I know now that he's right. I was completely fooled by Talbot. What I imagined to be the signs of exciting flames of passion in the fellow were nothing but a false fire alarm. There wasn't a spark there, not even a smouldering cinder, not one tiny glowing ember of adventure or original thought. He was a well-meaning turnip. By birth a turnip. Nature had begun the job and his smothering family had taken over to round it off. Money, security, pampering —oh, he was harmless enough. But who wants to marry a turnip?

Then came the ad. It was in the *Overseas Employment* section and why I glanced at that column on that particular morning, I'll never know. I guess Providence had just picked me out to play a major rôle in one of her sadistic little diversions. The ad. read: "A New Zealand family wish to employ a well-spoken young English woman twenty to thirty years as guardian-companion to two school-age children, for a period of three months. Driving licence desirable. Good speech essential. Fare to and from Auckland will be paid. Salary negotiable . . . For further details write to E. Sullivan, care New Zealand House, Haymarket, London." Just like that, spelt out in full, with none of the usual abbreviations like drv.lic. and so on. It must have cost a packet to insert in the *Telegraph*.

Well, I drove my father's car when I could get my hands on it and I was twenty-eight and I didn't drop my 'h's or slur my words. So it set me thinking. It offered a way out, because if I went abroad for three months Talbot the Turnip would find another girl and he wouldn't be hurt. He's not the steadfast type. I had a feeling that his parents had told him to get himself hitched and he'd grabbed at the first mug he found—me. If I wasn't around a replacement would

3

be simple, as I wouldn't be the only one lured by those dark mysterious eyes and high cheek-bones. So a trip by me to the other side of the world would let us both off the hook.

Of course, there'd be hundreds after a job like that. But what would it cost me to apply? One 16p stamp.

In three days I had an answer, giving an address and date for a personal interview.

In Kennington Road it was, and the queue stretched right down a stairway and into the street. I joined the end of the line and soon there were others behind me. Why couldn't they have chosen a short list from the applications instead of sending replies to so many? To fill in the time I tried to calculate the postage it had cost them. The girl in front of me joined in and we did some mental arithmetic together. She was better looking than I. I don't have buck teeth or warts and I look all right when I'm painted and polished. But she was a smasher, with big dark eyes and a lovely smile and a delightful

Scottish accent. What hope in the world had I?

The queue was moving, really moving. I stepped up several yards in two minutes. Then I saw that the girls were coming out of another doorway of the same building, further down the street. And still the line moved, steadily, as if we filing through a toll gate or the Express-Six-Items-Only checkout at a supermarket. Now I was on the stairs, then the landing, and I could see those ahead of me going one by one into a room. None came out the same way and just for a moment I thought of white slavery and wondered whether some of them were being dropped down a hole into a barge waiting below on an underground canal leading to the Thames. I had no way of knowing if as many came out as went in. But then I was up to the door myself, a voice called "Next!" and I entered.

It was a small room where a tired-looking man sat behind a desk. I was not asked my name. I was not invited to sit.

"'Morning," he said. "Read that aloud,

please." He pushed a sheet of paper towards me.

It was something about the predicted recovery of the economic situation in the United States. I stumbled over it, hesitated, stopped and started.

"Hm," he commented when I'd finished. "Try this." He handed me a copy of *The Times*. "Anywhere," he said. "Just read."

I read, choosing paragraphs at random and leaving out sentences if they contained technical terms I might mispronounce. After a few minutes he said, "That's enough. Driver's licence?"

"Yes."

"Free to leave next week?"

"I'm working. I have to give a fortnight's notice."

"Sit down."

I sat. I was glad to, because my legs had gone all pulpy and weak at the sudden hope that I had a chance. I'd already been in the room longer than any of the others I'd seen enter it.

"You fulfil the conditions," he said.

6

"Your speech will do. Best so far anyway and I can't sit here all day. You look a sensible, practical young woman." I was glad I'd removed my scarlet nail polish and worn the navy blue coat and skirt. "But I must have a firm decision. Do you want the job or don't you?"

I'm all for quick decisions and the sort I make are firm. "I do."

"You have a passport?"

"I brought it."

"Excellent." He looked impressed at my foresight and confidence, so I didn't tell him it just happened to be in my best handbag, which I hadn't used since my trip to Brittany last summer.

"I have character references, too." I began to get them out but he waved them away.

"Your passport, please." He examined it, wrote down its number and date and place of issue, then handed it back. "Give notice tomorrow. Fill in this form. You'll fly Tuesday 22nd November, arriving Auckland New Zealand on Thursday 24th. Your ticket will be sent to you."

I filled in the questionnaire—name, address, date of birth, present place of employment and so on—then gave it back to him and found myself dismissed. "Thank you, good morning," he said and gestured to the door.

But I was curious and paused on the way out. "Would you please tell me why I got the job over all the other candidates? I'd really like to know."

I hoped he'd say he'd chosen me for my attractive personality or engaging appearance. He didn't. "Your voice. Good enunciation. BBC. Pure vowel sounds. No regional accent. University education?"

"One year at Somerville."

"It's done the job. My clients want their children to imitate speech like yours."

His clients sounded a bit snobby to me. But I'd made my decision. I was out in the street before I remembered he hadn't told me the salary. No matter. They'd have to feed and lodge me. Who cared about wages?

The next two weeks are rather confused in my memory—buying clothes, reasoning with parents, listening to predictions of my future. Aunt Heather said I'd have to wear a grass skirt and unsuccessfully tried to order one through Marks and Spencer. Uncle George advised me to take a few coloured beads to appease the Maoris, the woman next door said to be sure to pack dresses with wide let-out seams because New Zealanders lived on a diet of roast lamb with lashings of thick cream on top. The girls in the office wanted me to send them back a boomerang, until they found that there are over a thousand miles between New Zealand and the nearest boomerang.

Then the day came with its final goodbyes. Talbot was among those who came to the airport to see me off and at the last moment he thrust into my hand a framed coloured photograph of himself. Just what he *would* do! Not a tempting box of Swiss chocolates for the long tiring voyage, or a bottle of French perfume to soothe the weary brow, but what he considered would best gladden the heart of any woman bound for savage unknown shores —a broadly smiling picture of Talbot the Turnip.

A long flight in the economy section of a jumbo jet, squashed up with four hundred others like a herd of cattle on its way to the meat works. Being fed at intervals, trying to sleep, watching a third of a film on the third of the screen that was visible, an hour's stop at Singapore, walking round the terminal there in the middle of the night, up and down, up and down, back in the plane, another meal, another third of a film, and finally landing. Sitting in the plane for ten minutes while an official sprayed us all for ticks—it's habit, I guess. They're more used to sheep here than people—and at last down one of those corrugated cardboard tubes into a building saying

Welcome to New Zealand have your passport and immigration card ready there are heavy penalties for failing to declare goods bought overseas Health and Immigration wait here until called Agriculture and Fisheries queue behind the white line Amnesty Box this is your last chance there are heavy penalties . . .

When I'd negotiated all the check-points, collected my luggage and passed through Customs, I followed the instructions given me in London by finding the Enquiry Counter and telling the attendant my name. She picked up her microphone and paged a Mr. Bronson.

2

"MISS PAMELA MARTIN? I'm Maxwell Bronson."

He held out his hand. He was a large, jovial-looking man of late middle age, with a square solid face and a prosperous middle. His hair was thinning on top and his forehead was lined but an air of good humour and reliability appealed to me. He welcomed me, hoped I'd had a good trip, took up my two cases and led me across a car park to a modern blue Renault. I carried my overnight bag. Then he took that, too, and put it in the boot of the car with the other cases before he opened the door for me to climb in.

It was mid-morning and the sun was already strong as we drove away from the airport. I had an impression of open spaces, green paddocks, horses, low, rough buildings, corrugated iron sheds, wide streets with ugly rows of telegraph poles each side, roadside stalls advertising vegetables, varied residential dwellings— mainly wooden bungalows, all colours, each one detached from its neighbours— a railway yard, concrete walled factories, glimpses of water and yachts. Much of it looked primitive and scruffy after the smoothly cultivated English landscape. Mr. Bronson talked pleasantly as he drove, pointing out landmarks and commenting on the fine day. "I'm sure you're going to enjoy your stay in our country, Miss Martin. We have a very comfortable home in the best part of Auckland, the suburb of Parnell, close to the city centre. We had to pay over two hundred thousand for the property but it's what we wanted."

In England you don't tell a person you've just met how much you paid for your living quarters, but I found out later that in New Zealand you do. It's like stating your qualifications or saying "We're a branch of the *Nottingham* Birketts, you know," just to reassure the person you're speaking to that you're socially acceptable.

"What exactly are my duties, Mr. Bronson?"

"Oh, just to be with our two girls. Go about with them during the school holidays which start at the end of this week."

"How old are they?"

"Charis is fifteen. She'll be sitting School Cert. next year. Diella is thirteen. Just had her first year at secondary."

It seemed to me that the last thing two teenagers would want in their holidays was an older woman tagging along spoiling the fun. He must have guessed what I was thinking because he added, "Not all the time, of course. But you'll be in the house with them when they're home and I'd like you to accompany them on a few trips. Take them in the car, as they're too young to drive yet. They're friendly youngsters and I know you'll get on with them. They're looking forward to meeting you. They would have liked to come to the airport with me but I wouldn't let them miss school. It was because of the girls that we moved from Glendowie. We had a beautiful home there but we wanted to be in the grammar zone."

"Oh?" I didn't like to ask what that was. I had a sudden vision of all the householders in Parnell brushing up their *lay, laid, lain* before breakfast each morning and grappling the component parts of their infinitives together with hoops of steel.

"They'll be happy to show you around Auckland," he went on, "and Wesley can go with you if you don't mind. He's a bit of a trial for the girls alone, poor Wes."

"A dog?"

He laughed. "No, Wesley is my unmarried brother. He makes his home with us now. There's no harm in him but he's just . . . not . . . quite . . . oh, you'll see. How do you like our new bridge over the Manukau Harbour? Opened at the beginning of this year. It took ten years to complete because shortly after they'd started the workers went on strike and it stood out for years against the skyline as a symbol of Union power and obstruction. Ugly in its unfinished state but a point of interest to strangers and a subject for amateur photographers. I believe one view of it took first prize in the Easter Show for three years running. Well, it's built now but instead of the estimated price it's cost us poor taxpayers millions more. I hope that doesn't put you off our country?"

"On the contrary," I assured him, "it makes me feel at home."

"That's Onehunga on the right . . . we go through the Mt. Roskill area now . . . here's Mt. Eden . . . that's the Mount, see? A good restaurant at the top and fine views over the city. You must go one day. Into Newmarket now, one of our busy shopping centres . . . this is Parnell Road . . . down here, round this corner . . . here we are. Our street." He turned into a wide, tree-lined avenue and then up a short concrete drive to a large wooden bungalow, painted dark brown and white. It stood on a gently sloping section of nearly half an acre. I saw fruit trees, flower beds and well-kept lawns.

As we pulled up a woman came down the front steps to meet us. She was tall, thin, willowy, with a long pale face and elaborately waved blonde hair. I put her age in the mid-forties. "Miss Martin?" she said. "I'm Fiona Bronson. Welcome to our home. I hope you're not too tired after your long trip. Do come up. Max will bring your luggage but I'm sure the first thing you'd like is a cup of tea."

New Zealanders have this Thing about the English drinking tea all day and brewing a potful as first reaction to any crisis. I guess it's watching *Coronation Street* that does it. But as a matter of fact I did want a cup, even before a shower. I followed her up the flight of concrete steps into the main entrance hall. Because of the slope of the section, a large double garage, workshop and billiard room had been built at ground level in front. The living portion of the bungalow was above them, the back leading directly out to the rear garden.

17

"This way." She led me into what they call the lounge, the accepted term over here for living-room. It was spacious, airy and light, with comfortable chairs and sofas, a baby grand piano, a television set and a stereo. The wide front windows had a view of the sea, sparkling blue and dotted with yachts.

An old lady was sitting in one of the velvet-covered armchairs. "My mother-in-law," said Mrs. Bronson. A pair of bright eyes regarded me fixedly. They wore no glasses and it was difficult to know whether she was giving me a piercing intelligent summing-up or just a myopic stare. She nodded but did not speak.

Mrs. Bronson made the tea herself. There were no servants. I found out next day that a woman came to clean once a week and an odd-job man mowed the lawns and did some of the heavier gardening, but like most New Zealand women, Mrs. Bronson did nearly all the work herself. "Do sit down, Miss Martin. I shan't be long."

I sat in an easy chair near the old lady

and tried to make conversation but my remarks about the sunshine and the view and the drive from the airport were received without comment. It was a relief when Mrs. Bronson brought in the tea and started chatting. Her voice was soft, her manner friendly but rather vague. "Please call me Fiona. It will be less confusing with my mother-in-law here. And you're Pamela, aren't you?" As we drank our tea she asked about my trip, my family, the weather when I left England. We admired the view and she pointed out Rangitoto, the inactive volcano which stands in the harbour and which Aucklanders are so proud of that they adopt it as their trademark. I liked her but all the time she spoke I had a feeling that she was not giving me her whole attention. Something else was on her mind.

Then Mr. Bronson came in. "I've taken your bags to the flat," he told me, "but I'm very sorry. I dropped your overnight bag—trying to carry too much at once— and spilled your talcum powder all over the lino in the kitchenette. I washed it up but I'm afraid there'll be some in your bag as well."

I was puzzled. "I didn't bring any talcum powder."

"Well, face-powder. I don't know about these matters. I hope it hasn't damaged anything in your bag."

"I didn't have face-powder in my bag. I use a compact and it's here in my handbag."

"Face-powder's well out of date, Max," said his wife. "Whatever *have* you spilled?"

The older Mrs. Bronson, who had not said a word while she drank her tea, now spoke up sharply, "What have you done, Maxwell?"

He ignored her and addressed me. "Perhaps you'd better come and see." Fiona and I followed him out to the hall and then through a door into what were to be my quarters.

"It's a granny flat," explained Fiona. "We had it built for Max's mother. But she's a bit frail to be on her own now so she's moved in with us and the flat is usually unoccupied. We thought it would be ideal for you. There's a door opening on to the back garden, so you can come and go as you please. Your own bathroom and a little kitchenette. Of course, you'll have your meals with us, but you may like to make yourself a cup of tea in private sometimes or entertain friends."

I looked around with amazement. "It's perfectly lovely. I hadn't expected anything like this."

"Did you think we'd lodge you in a loft above the garden shed?" laughed Mr. Bronson. He had put my bag on the kitchen table. It was half-open and there was some white powder on the edges of the zip. I opened it fully and found, on top of the other articles, a small round cardboard box with its lid off and the powdery contents all over my cardigan, and my book and Talbot's photograph. I hurriedly turned my back on the others, took Talbot out and slipped him into the pocket of the suit I was wearing. Somehow I didn't want them to see

21

Talbot. He'd have to be disposed of, poor guy. Into that blue harbour among the yachts or down the crater of the volcano. I'd find somewhere. Then I picked out the box and showed it to them. "This isn't mine. I don't know what it is or where it came from."

Mr. Bronson suddenly looked serious. "How did it get into your bag?"

"I've no idea. I've never seen it before. Look, it has a number on the lid. No label. What is it?"

"Someone's face-powder?" suggested Mr. Bronson.

His wife said, "In a pill box? Don't be silly, Max."

He was frowning. "I think you'd better wash your hands, Miss Martin. It could be insecticide, accidentally dropped into your bag." He explained to me, "New Zealand is predominantly an agricultural country and we're proud of our clean record. The authorities take elaborate precautions to keep out any animal diseases or crop infestation, and rightly so. If foot-and-mouth got in, for instance, it could cost the farmers, or rather us taxpayers, millions of dollars, and even ruin our export trade. If you've visited a farm before you arrive in New Zealand you'll even have to have your shoes disinfected at the airport to guard against the possible entry of any bacteria which might affect crops or livestock. This looks to me as if it's a box of some substance used for that purpose and if so it could be highly lethal, because to be packed in such a small container as this, it must be heavily concentrated. I think, with your permission, the best place for it is our back yard incinerator. I tell you what, though. Just to satisfy our curiosity, I'll keep a little bit and have it analysed."

He took a paper out of his pocket—some receipt or invoice by the look of it—tipped a small portion of what was still in the box onto the paper and then folded it up carefully and put it in his wallet. Then he took the little box. "Go and wash your hands straight away, will you please, Miss Martin? I'll be back in a jiffy. He left by the back door which led to the garden.

When I returned from the bathroom—thick towels there, bath salts, shampoo, hair spray and lovely scented soap. What dears they were to treat me so generously!—he was coming back carrying a bucket and a piece of cloth. "Well, that's burned," he told us. "Now your bag, Miss Martin. Think me mad if you like but I'd prefer to take no risks. Do you mind if we empty it and wipe it out?"

"Of course I don't. There's not much in it. Just a book and a cardigan and slippers to wear in the plane. Oh, and some tissues."

He already had the bag open and was emptying the contents. "My hands are already contaminated so I'd better do it for you. Book . . ." He wiped the cover and edges carefully with the wet rag. "Better wash the cardigan. I'll pop it in the handbasin with some water and you can do it later."

"He's not really crazy," his wife assured me while he was in the bathroom.

24

"If it's concentrated insecticide, it's really dangerous. Even a speck could kill. And it *is* likely to be that, because they dip and spray lavishly. They have to. We had a narrow escape this year from that awful fruit-fly. They found a live maggot on Australian tomatoes that some idiot smuggled in."

Mr. Bronson came back. "I rinsed it once and I've left it in the basin for you to do the rest. Tissues . . . play safe. I'll burn them. Slippers . . . you have them in a plastic packet so they should be all right. Take them out, will you, while I hold the container open? I'll dispose of it. That's the lot. Now I'll clean your bag out for you and dry it in the sun. I'll take it outside to do it."

"I'm very grateful for all your trouble. I simply can't understand how that stuff got into my bag." Why would anyone put a box of poison in among my things? And when could it have been done? Were such occurrences common in this country? At least it had been discovered and dealt with in time. I admired the efficient way in which Mr. Bronson had handled the matter and didn't like to think what I'd have done, or what might have happened to me, if I'd been alone when I opened the bag.

"What would you like to do now?" asked Fiona when her husband had left us. "See round the property or unpack?"

"I'd like to shower and change first, please. Your weather is so much warmer than ours. I'm far too hot in this woollen suit."

"A good idea. Have you everything you need? Take your time. Come through when you're ready and I'll show you the house and the garden."

I hung up my tweed suit—I wouldn't need *that* for a while—showered and changed into a light summer dress. Then I went back to the main part of the house and Fiona showed me round. The rooms were large, all comfortably, expensively furnished, with thick pile carpet even in the bathrooms, a mahogany suite in the spacious dining-room, beautiful rich curtains throughout, original paintings on the walls of the lounge and hall. I judge painting with a taste quite unhampered by any knowledge of art or technique and these I found I liked, because I could understand them. They were mainly views of country landscape, beaches, flowers or groups of trees. Several were signed *F. Elliott*, which I later learned was Fiona's maiden name.

A large grandfather clock stood in the hall but for some reason I took an instant dislike to it, perhaps because it was not a real traditional one with weights, like the ancient, dignified heirloom in my parents' home. It was a modern wind-up job with a pendulum of stainless steel. The two key holes resembled evil eyes and the *Tempus fugit* printed beneath them formed the curve of a malicious, sneering mouth, which scowled at me the way my boss had when I'd given him notice. It had an uneven tick, too. Tick, ger-TOCK, pause . . . tick, ger-TOCK, pause . . . tick, ger-TOCK. . . I was to grow to loathe that clock, but I didn't know it at the time. I just felt we didn't take to each other.

Underfloor central electric heating kept the house warm, Fiona told me, though at this time of year it was turned off. Every comfort, every convenience, was there. Microwave double eye-level oven, dishmaster under the bench, waste-disposal unit, the latest washing machine and drier in the laundry, refrigerator, deep freeze —they had it all. Then we went outside and looked at the garden, the ornamental shrubs, the trees, the large swimming pool with tiled surround and sides, the lounge swing, the barbecue area, the wrought iron weatherproof table and chairs. The back section was overlooked by other houses higher up the hillside but trees and a garden shed afforded privacy. It was all well appointed, tastefully arranged and carefully maintained, yet I couldn't help feeling it was in the wrong setting. It should have had rolling downs below it, a grassy slope leading to a little brook. I tried to imagine the house surrounded by the smooth orderly beauty of an English landscape and felt a little homesick.

I unpacked after that, then found Fiona preparing lunch. When I offered to help she said, "That's not at all necessary. It's not what you're here for."

"I'm not sure what I *am* here for."

Fiona looked up, straight at me, and said, "Neither am I." Then, as if regretting her words, she added quickly, "You could help me with the salad, if you really don't mind. Oh, here's Wesley. He's been taking Chief for a walk. Did Max tell you about Wesley? He's not quite . . ."

Wesley came in. He had a large head, reddish hair and a look of wonderment in big brown doggy eyes. His shoulders were bent and in the first few minutes I saw that his motor coordination was not normal. But his face was gentle. A melancholy in the brown eyes contradicted the cheerful upturn of the corners of his mouth and I felt sorry for him. Did he know he wasn't quite? He looked down at his hands now and then as if surprised to find them so clumsy. Fiona introduced us and he said, "Hallo. Glad to meet you," in a pleasant voice. There was no speech defect.

"Did you have a nice walk, Wesley?" asked Fiona, as one would to a small child.

"Yes, I went three times round the reserve." He was looking at me as he spoke and I wondered what he thought of a stranger invading the house. No, he wasn't quite. You could see that. But there was something appealing about him, just as there was about the friendly, tail-wagging spaniel he'd left on the doorstep. I was introduced to Chief, who licked my hand in welcome.

We had lunch out on the terrace over-looking the harbour and my eyes kept turning to the shimmering blue water. Mr. Bronson had a yacht moored there, you could just see a part of the stern "behind that yellow keeler, see?" He would take me and the girls out one day in the holidays. Did I do any yachting at home? The talk was superficial. Wesley said little, old Mrs. Bronson even less, but Fiona and her husband spoke of Auckland, of their visits to England, of aeroplane flights and of their two children. There was no reference to the powder in my bag. After lunch Mr. Bronson went back to work. He was a company director, Fiona explained, and worked long hours. He'd taken time off to meet me at the airport but I gathered he was involved in several leading import companies and was kept very busy most days.

Fiona took me out later in her own car, a Mitsubishi Mirage. Mrs. Bronson refused an invitation to come, but Wesley and Chief sat on the back seat, talking more to each other than to us. Fiona drove under oak trees in a domain, along the waterfront, up to the top of Mt. Eden and through residential suburbs. She invited me to take the wheel after a while, as I would have the use of the car when she didn't want it herself. It was easy to handle and I enjoyed the feel of it.

The two girls were home from school when we returned. They ran out when they heard the car. "Is she here?"—"Has she come?" They were naturally curious to see what they'd been landed with for the next three months.

We climbed out of the Mirage and they were introduced to me. Charis, the fifteen-year-old, had long fair hair and a pale face like her mother. She had her mother's dreaminess, too, and the same air of hearing what you say while thinking of something else. The younger, Diella, was darker in skin and hair and more lively in nature. I liked them both.

They were not shy. As we walked towards the house Diella took me by the arm. "Dad says we have to learn to talk posh like you. We've got to listen to you and copy you, so you'll have to talk an awful lot. Let's take her out in the garden, Charis, and make her talk."

"She's not a tame parrot," said Fiona. "She'll come with you only if she feels like it. She's had a long plane ride and may prefer to rest."

"Of course I feel like it," I assured them. "Show me the way."

We sat on the chairs under the copper beech tree near the pool, while they told me about their school, their friends, their hobbies. They asked about my own family, London Bridge, had I shaken hands with the Queen, were people still shut up in the Tower of London, was there any countryside left in Britain or did the cities all meet up together now. . . some of the girls at school had had a trip overseas but Dad said *they* had to wait until they were through High School . . .

Fiona Bronson cooked the dinner and did not allow me to help. When Mr. Bronson came home we all sat in the lounge and continued to chat over a glass of sherry before the meal. The girls were told about the powder in my bag. "Oh, how awful if you'd licked your fingers! You might have just got here and then died a horrible death, writhing in agony and we'd have had detective inspectors and fingerprint men . . . it *would* have been rather fun." There was a wistful note in Diella's voice but she went on, "I'm glad you didn't, though," and I was pleased to know that my live company had been assessed as slightly more acceptable than an entertaining police investigation over a corpse.

"We break up tomorrow," said Charis. "It's awfully early this year because we started early."

"That's not why," said Diella. "Old Scraggytop told us in Maths that it's because of cutting the Easter break and only having one day at mid-term break."

"That wouldn't be enough, silly. They must have done us out of the Monday in the May holidays and a few others. Dad, you won't forget about Waitangi, will you, and the Bay of Islands? Pam would love it up there."

"We'll see she has a really good time while she's here," said their father, and smiled at me.

I leaned back and listened to the chatter. I could hardly believe my luck in finding myself in such pleasant surroundings among such friendly, agreeable people. The next three months held promise of one long holiday.

That was the last care-free day I was ever to have in New Zealand.

3

THE next day, Friday, was the break-up of the school year and the girls were home by lunchtime. I had spent the morning finishing my unpacking, talking to Fiona and Wesley and inspecting the garden. Fiona refused to let me help with the housework but I pulled a few weeds out of the rose-bed. Mrs. Bronson came out and stood by me once so I made an effort to win her approval. "We have the King's Ransom and the Sabrina and the Vagabonde in our own garden at home," I said, showing off, "but this one is new to me. What is it?"

"I have no idea," she said curtly. "Does it matter?"

"Do you like gardening, Mrs. Bronson?"

"No. Why should I? I don't know why you're messing your hands up like that.

They can afford to get someone in to do it."

"I thought it would help Fiona."

"Fiona's a fool in some ways. She doesn't have to work as hard as she does. You've missed some oxalis at the base of that scarlet one."

I was glad when the girls came running round the side of the house. "School's over. Seven weeks' holiday! What you been doing, Pam? Why are you weeding the garden? Did you tell her to, Gran? Come for a swim before lunch, Pam. You haven't tried our pool yet, have you? We just had it put in last year. It's neat, eh?"

I agreed when I tried it. It was not merely "neat", it was luxurious, blue-tiled, heated to a temperature of 68°, over six feet at the deep end and about fifty feet long. I was glad I swam well and could just race Charis from one end to the other.

Fiona suggested we spend the afternoon meeting other members of the family. She had two sisters within walking distance and visiting them would give me a chance to look at the district and to examine more closely the construction of the wooden bungalows I'd expressed surprise at the day before. I didn't like to say they resembled painted barns but they looked so flimsy and temporary compared with the solid houses at home that I asked how long they were good for.

They laughed at me. "Some of the early kauri villas are over a hundred years old," said Fiona.

"They don't really blow over," said Diella. "They even stand earthquakes. You don't have earthquakes, do you? Oh, wouldn't it be fabulous if we had one while you're here—not a big one, of course, to kill people, just a little one to rattle things and sway the lights and throw ornaments off shelves?"

"No, it would not," said her mother. "But you should take Pam to Rotorua one day and she can watch some activity there."

"Oh yes, we must. And Waitomo caves and all sorts of places. You'd like to see our geysers, wouldn't you, Pam? It's going to be great having you here and using Mum's car. And Dad says he's going to take a few days off after Christmas and we'll all go up to Waitangi and stay at the hotel there so that you can see the Treaty House and the flag pole that Honi Heke used to chop down each time they put it up and there's super beaches up past there—good surf, we've got a spare surf board for you but we haven't got a wind surfer yet because Dad says they're dangerous, only *I* don't think they are. Susan, that's one of my school mates, *she's* got one, she got it for her birthday . . ."

As we walked along to visit their aunts, they chatted all the way. Charis was the more serious one and at times pointed out landmarks in the distance. "See, that's the new Sheraton Hotel. You can just see the roof. Over there's the Mt. Eden Gardens. We'll take you one day. They're awfully pretty. Look, you can see the Harbour Bridge now."

I told them, "Some of my friends in

England thought the Harbour Bridge linked Australia and New Zealand."

"That would be the Sydney Harbour Bridge," said Charis. "It's a bit more famous than ours. Do English people really think we're a part of Australia? Gosh, how *awful!* It's miles away. Three hours in a jet plane."

There was no resentment apparent at having a chaperon, if such was my rôle, nor at their father's wish that they copy my manner of speech. Occasionally Diella would come out with a remark such as "Whoops, I didn't say that right, did I? Not Tuesdee. Tuesdi. How's that?"

Just two nice, normal, friendly girls politely entertaining a visitor. Since my speech was of such importance I paid special attention to it, trying not to slur my words or swallow their endings. Was that to be my only duty? Driving the girls around in the modern, easily handled Mirage would be a pleasure, as was strolling like this in the mild sunshine.

Aunt Vera Elliott lived in Grafton, in a "unit", the end flat in a block of four owner-occupied ones, built of brick and all alike. Each had a garage in front and a garden at the back and apart from being one-storeyed were more like English dwellings than anything I'd yet seen. Miss Elliott is a spinster and even before I was told I knew she was a schoolteacher. For one thing, the strain of her profession showed up on her face. Charis had told me she was forty-five but she looked ten years older. Dozens of small creases fanned out from her eyes and deep lines marked her brow and the sides of her mouth. And then she wore such unbecoming clothes—the conventional disguise of those intellectuals who are ashamed of being brighter than the other members of their family and so dress themselves in shapeless, colourless clothes no woman of sense would be seen in.

I liked her, though. She was refreshingly direct in her manner. "So you're the young lady Maxwell has brought twelve thousand miles to teach my nieces not to say 'Hiya'?" She appeared amused at the thought. "Come in. Sit down. I'll make coffee."

She taught at a state secondary school, she told me. She'd been to England three times and was planning another trip, a long stay, when she retired at fifty. She'd made friends over there and she knew the area of Richmond where I lived. We talked of the river, the theatre, and a small café which had been newly opened last time she was there. It was still doing business, I was able to tell her, although it had changed hands twice. When she came over again we'd have lunch there together.

When we left her we walked half a mile further on to see Aunt Mary Mersey, who lived in a white bungalow on a small, well-kept section. She was older than Fiona and Vera, a plump cheerful housewife with a wide smiling mouth, the sort of woman you visualise in a kitchen with a spotless white apron on and a patch of flour on one cheek. She wasn't dressed that way when we called. She wore boots and too-tight slacks and carried a garden trowel. She kissed the girls and gave me a hearty welcome before she kicked off her boots, threw the trowel down and led us inside.

I liked her, too. But I can't say the same of her husband, Harry. He was in the kitchen with two other men, sitting at a table covered with beer bottles, most of them empty. The girls looked a bit embarrassed and I gathered they had not expected him to be home on a Friday afternoon, but as we had gone in the back door, we had to walk through the kitchen to reach the lounge, and an introduction could not be avoided. Aunt Mary made it. He blinked bleary, red-rimmed eyes and said he was glad to see me. I didn't doubt it. Seeing anyone or anything in his present state would be a matter for self-congratulation. Then he muttered "Ces, Jim" and waved vaguely towards the other two men at the table. We passed through quickly and Aunt Mary shut the door behind us. Her husband owned his own business, she told me, a second-hand car sales, and had taken the afternoon off.

"Are you terribly homesick, my dear? How brave of you to come all that way. And so kind!"

"I wanted to come, Mrs. Mersey. There were hundreds after the job."

"Oh dear, is that a fact? Conditions must be far worse than they tell us in the news. Well, we must feed you up while you're here, mustn't we, girls? Build up your resistance and send you back fit to cope."

I didn't argue. At a later date I could give her some facts about Britain, but I guessed she would remain unconvinced that anyone would voluntarily leave friends and family unless driven by hardship or some private urgent reason. She was a home lover herself, content with her house, her garden and her social circle. I thought to myself that if I had been married to such a drunken slob as Harry I'd have fled the country long ago, but some women are born to accept suffering with patient, cheerful resignation. She gave every appearance of being satisfied with her lot in this life. She was knitting

Diella a cardigan and the talk soon turned to colours, patterns and the appalling price of pure wool in the shops.

We went out by the front door, avoiding the men in the kitchen, but before we left the premises she showed us round her small garden, pointed out the salvias she had just planted and gave us some seedling cabbages for Fiona. "If you've nothing better to do, come to lunch on Monday," she suggested. "I must get to know Pamela better." We accepted. Lunch, I noted, and a weekday, when her husband would hopefully be out of the house. Poor Aunt Mary.

Then we walked back home. "They're nice, aren't they?" said Charis. "Aunt Vera and Aunt Mary, I mean." She was excluding her uncle.

"I like them both very much," I said truthfully. "But why don't you copy *their* speech? Your Aunt Vera has no trace of a New Zealand accent. She'd pass for a native in England. I feel I'm here under false pretences. I can't really understand why your father wanted to employ an English person at all."

"Diella and I started it ourselves," Charis told me. "Dad was always growling about the way we talk and saying he should have sent us to a private school and why couldn't New Zealanders speak decent English. You see, he's been over to England lots of times."

Diella went on, "So we said what about sending us on a trip to England then, so that we could learn to speak nicely? But that didn't work. We have to wait until we've both been through High School, then he's promised us a trip. So one of us said all right then, why not import a few English people? We didn't mean it, of course, and he got annoyed and told us not to be silly and we weren't taking heed of what he said and good speech was so important . . ."

"And if he heard us say 'dincha' again, so much the worse for us."

Diella giggled. "Only the next day he gave us a real surprise. He said he'd been thinking the matter over and our suggestion was actually a sound one. It wouldn't be a bad idea to provide us with an English companion for a while, one who spoke naturally but well, not plum-in-the-mouth, but just clearly with good vowel sounds. And before we knew it, he'd arranged to have an ad. put in overseas and one of his contacts in London was to choose someone. Oh gosh, Pammy, we thought it might be an old fogey with her hair in a bun."

"The advertisement said twenty to thirty years of age," I told them. "But I was afraid that at twenty-eight, I *would* be considered an old fogey."

"You're not a bit," said Diella, and I knew she meant it.

As on the previous day, we sat out on the terrace before dinner. Fiona and Wesley joined us, Mrs. Bronson sat just inside the ranchsliders, where she could hear the conversation and contribute if she felt inclined. The sun was low now but there was no wind. The air was warm and a faint scent of jasmine came up from the front garden. The girls began testing me on what they thought I should by now have learned. "What's that white building, Pam? That's right, the museum. And the tall brick one on the left? . . . But we *told* you. Don't you remember?"

"Who's teaching whom?" I retorted. "Let me hear you say 'remember' again. Not 'remyeember' this time."

Fiona laughed. "That's right, Pam. Don't let them bully you."

Then Mr. Bronson came home and dropped the bombshell which was to blast into fragments the pleasure of my stay. We saw the car drive in, heard him garage it and then he came up the steps. After greeting the others, he came straight up to me. "Miss Martin, that sample of powder I took—I had it analysed this morning. It's heroin."

"Heroin?" I echoed in astonishment.

"Scag? Junk?" said Diella excitedly. "Oh, what fun! We had a talk on that in Liberal Studies last week."

"Are you sure, Max?" asked Fiona.

"What's that you're saying, Maxwell?" Old Mrs. Bronson had risen and was standing at the ranchslider door. "I don't believe it."

"Unfortunately it's true," he said. "There's no doubt about it. Someone must have slipped it into Miss Martin's bag." He turned to me again. "You didn't . . . that is, you weren't . . . did anyone ask you to bring it over for them, as a favour? Without telling you what it was, of course?"

He was offering me a way out, in case I had smuggled it in. "No," I replied indignantly. "I'd never seen it before, as I told you. I wouldn't have accepted anything like that."

"No, no, of course not. I just thought I'd better make sure." The look he gave me indicated clearly that he was *not* sure. In spite of my protestation, there was a small doubt in his mind. I reminded myself that I was a stranger to him and must not take offence at his mistrust.

"Was there anyone on the plane whom you recognised?" he asked.

"I didn't know a soul."

"Did anyone borrow your bag? Handle

it for you? Offer to carry it? Did you leave it alone at anytime?"

"No one touched it as far as I know. I left it by my seat once or twice on the plane when I went to the toilet."

"Who were you sitting next to?"

"A woman. But we hardly spoke. Anyway, I put my slippers back in the bag just before we landed at Auckland and the box wasn't there then. I'd have seen it."

"Not if it were at the bottom of your bag, below the other articles. I must have tipped the contents when I dropped it, bringing the box to the surface. Perhaps it was put in after you landed, when someone wanted to get rid of it in a hurry. When you were waiting for your cases, for instance, you'd have your bag on the ground beside you, and would be pre-occupied watching the conveyor belt."

"Leave the girl alone, Maxwell," said his mother sharply. I was grateful to her. The news that I'd been carrying heroin had been a shock, as she must have realised, and I could not just then think clearly. I didn't want to be questioned.

"We have to find out, Mother," said Mr. Bronson. "Do you realise how serious this is, Miss Martin? I think we'd better go to the police station and report the matter. That way you'll put yourself in the clear. I have an appointment this evening but I'll take you tomorrow morning, if that suits you." I knew the last phrase was a concession to courtesy. I'd go if he had to drag me there. But in fact I saw that it would be the best thing to do.

"You needn't have been so fussy about washing the bag out for poison, then," said Fiona. "Thank goodness it wasn't insecticide."

Her husband looked at her with a worried frown. "I wish to God it had been." Then he changed the subject, asking the girls what we'd done today and how their mother's sisters were. They chattered away to him and all seemed normal again.

But during dinner I knew it was not. I noticed a sort of restraint in his attitude

51

to me which had not been there the day before. I could hardly blame him. He didn't know me and he would feel responsible for letting his girls associate with someone who possibly—just possibly—might be involved in smuggling drugs. No, I didn't blame him at all. I was more concerned at Fiona's lack of concern. As for old Mrs. Bronson, she looked at me with those bright beady eyes of hers and I couldn't tell what she was thinking. It was an uncomfortable meal.

The evening was strained also. Diella brought the matter up once and her father again changed the subject with noticeable haste. I asked to be excused to go to bed early and permission was readily granted. In spite of a comfortable bed and a pure down duvet, I slept badly.

The next morning Mr. Bronson drove me down town to the police headquarters. "It's better to go to the main office and it's the only one fully open on Saturdays." He still had a tiny bit of the powder, now in a chemist's envelope. When he explained our business we were taken to a special department which deals with drugs. Two men were in the room. Mr. Bronson produced the envelope and the chemist's report, gave a brief account of what had happened, how he had discovered the powder and the steps he'd taken when he thought it to be insecticide. They disapproved his actions. He should have kept the container. Then they turned on me and the questions began.

They asked me again and again about boarding the plane, what I'd done, where I'd gone, who sat next to me, how often did I leave my bag unattended, was I sure I looked in it after the period at the air terminal in Singapore? Could I not have overlooked a small box? Over and over they asked the same questions, as if giving me a chance to make a different answer. I had to state the names and addresses of all my close relatives in England, where I'd worked, how long, what I'd done before that, what school I had attended . . . on and on and on. Of course they examined my passport, too, and noted its particulars. It was nearly two hours before they let us go and even when they thanked me for coming and assured me I'd done the right thing, I felt I'd been listed on a roll of suspected criminals.

"Well, that's over," said Mr. Bronson as he drove me back home.

I thanked him for giving up his morning. "It wasn't pleasant but I'm glad you made me go."

"I didn't find it pleasant either," he said. "I was in disgrace for destroying the container. Quite sarcastic, weren't they? But it seemed the most sensible course at the time. I hadn't a notion that it could have been a drug we were getting rid of."

"I'm still completely puzzled," I told him. "I've thought and thought and I can't see how that box could have been put into my bag without my knowledge."

"Drug pushers are cunning. There may be an incident which seemed so trivial to you at the time that it's slipped your memory. Someone leaning over you to take a photograph out the window?

Knocking against you in a crowd and apologising? Sitting beside you for a moment in the terminal building at Singapore? Well, never mind. You've reported it and you needn't worry about it any more. I *hope*," he added ominously.

The two girls were waiting eagerly to question me. "What happened, Pam? Where did you go? What did they say? Were there sniffer dogs there? Did they shine a bright light in your eyes?"

"They pulled out all her fingernails one by one," said Mr. Bronson with a false attempt at joviality. "How long to lunch? I'm starving."

He moved away and the girls resumed their questioning. I didn't feel like talking about it but I satisfied their curiosity and told them what I could remember. At least *they* didn't suspect me of anything except misadventure. I think Diella may even have envied me the unusual experience. And by answering all their questions I hoped to exhaust the subject and secure myself an afternoon free of it. It happened that way, too. We drove to the

North Shore after lunch and walked on the top of Mt. Victoria, looking down again, from another viewpoint, on to the blue harbour and the variety of little boats moored there. The heroin was not mentioned once.

There were visitors to dinner that evening and since I was a newcomer much attention was paid to me. What had I seen so far? What were my impressions? How had I spent my first couple of days? That was sufficient invitation for Diella to burst out with the story of the heroin. I saw her father about to stop her and then realise it was too late, for to curtail the account would only distort its importance. He let her finish and even added a few words of his own concerning the misguided persistence of the metropolitan police force.

None of the guests seemed to consider my experience very unusual. They swapped tales of mysterious parcels being popped into handbags, requests to take innocent-looking packages through customs. One had herself been asked to post a fat envelope at another airport and had been jittery all the way in the plane in case the customs seized it and found an uncut diamond or a pornographic booklet. One was warned all the time. If a stranger approached . . .

I assured them I had not been approached. Then we talked of other matters, such as the reactions to New Zealand life exhibited by a young woman visiting the country for the first time. Didn't I like the weather? What did I think of the beaches? Would I have the opportunity to visit the thermal regions?

After dinner, while I was helping the girls to stack the plates in the dishmaster, their father came into the kitchen and ordered them never again to mention the matter of the heroin before visitors. "It's not fair to Miss Martin. She doesn't want to have to go through the explanation every time someone calls." I was grateful to him.

4

I ACCOMPANIED the girls to church the next morning, the family service at 9.30. Their parents seldom went now, they told me, but insisted that Charis and Diella attend every Sunday. "Which is most unfair," complained Diella, "but they've promised that once we leave High School we can make up our own minds whether we go or not. And I don't really mind going because our Uncle Julian's the organist."

"That's Mum's brother," explained Charis. "He's nice. He plays what we ask him to for the voluntary, as long as it's something that won't offend the older parishioners."

"Like drinking songs or *Rip it up* or *Dracula's Tango*. He played *Always* once and *Kisses Sweeter than Wine* and even *Beat it*. But he refused our suggestion of *Back on the Chain Gang*. He said the vicar wouldn't mind but some of the congregation might and he didn't want to start a war."

"He says the vicar has enough to contend with soothing women who squabble over who does the flowers or how the seats should be arranged at a social."

Diella giggled. "He keeps a fish and chip shop and Dad doesn't like people to know. Charis and I call in now and then and he gives us potato patties but we don't tell Mum and Dad. We'll take you along to have some, too. You'll like him, honest you will."

"At least we can go to church in the car now you're here," said Charis. "It's a drag catching the bus and worse walking all the way."

"How far is it?"

"Miles and miles. Well, about one and a half, anyway. There are churches nearer but we go to St. Bernard's."

"Because your uncle is the organist?"

"Partly. And because Mum and Dad like the vicar. We do, too. He's a barmy old guy in some ways but he's interesting. He's only been there a few years but the first year he came Gran used to go to that church and she took a Bible Study group for him. They get on fine. He pops in to see her sometimes and they argue about things like garbage disposal and collection methods for the proposed Mt. Smart stadium. Anything. Last time they began on whether New Caledonia should have independence and ended with which timber to use for fence posts, and I don't think either of them knew much about that. Gran gets quite lively when he's here."

"He *must* be interesting." I felt respect for anyone who could get a spark out of that dour old woman.

So we drove to St. Bernard's, a wooden building which looked like a disused hen barn with an inverted ice-cream cone on top. I was getting used to these timber shacks but it still seemed strange for a church to be built that way. The construction could hardly be regarded as a symbol of permanence. It wasn't bad inside. The stained glass windows showed up brightly and the ends of the pews were intricately carved. The organ was playing as we entered. "Look, *there's* the top of our Uncle Julian's head," whispered Diella proudly.

"What's he playing?"

"The scherzo from Beethoven's Second. That's one of *his* favourites. He's taught us a lot about music. I used to think Beethoven was dull."

I enjoyed the service. The choir was good and I saw what they meant about the vicar. He was a big-built fellow with grey hair, getting old. At least sixty, I thought. But there was nothing senile about him. Some of the liturgy was chanted in a sing-song voice by a weedy young curate who gave the impression of being bowed down by the sins of the world—not his own, I guessed, just those of everyone else. But the old vicar was different. You'd think he was talking to you over the kitchen table, he spoke so naturally, yet clearly and forcibly. His sermon was short and contained none of those silly little funny stories that some of them *will* drag in to win the attention of their audience. He didn't joke at all. He spoke persuasively, vigorously and simply, giving you something meaty to think about without seeming to talk down to lower intelligences. I was quite impressed. What he said even took my mind temporarily off that nasty little box of heroin.

When the service was over the organist struck up the popular andante from Mozart's Concerto no. 21. Diella nudged me. "We made him promise to play that. He says it was written for piano and orchestra and isn't right on the organ, but he'd play it to keep us quiet."

"You think a lot of your Uncle Julian?"

"Rather. He's real spunky. Wait till you meet him."

As we filed out Charis introduced me to the vicar, Mr. Jarrett. Well, you know how it is sometimes? A floppy handshake and you guess the poor chap's thinking, This sheep's called Robinson or something. How many more of them? About twenty-five down, I reckon, forty to come . . . "so *nice* to see you, Mr. Robinson." Not this old boy. He couldn't stop to talk, with others coming on behind us, but his grip was firm and I had all his attention for those few brief minutes. When he said he hoped I'd enjoy my stay and that he'd see me again, I felt he really meant it.

"He's a batty old codger in some ways," said Diella as we walked to the car. "He talks all stiff and pompous and he keeps quoting the Bible, always coming out with some verse or other, usually one we've never heard of. I bet he makes half of them up."

"I bet he doesn't," said her sister. "And he's not a bit like that when you really want to talk to him. Not when you're worried about something and want his advice."

"I wouldn't know," said Diella. "I never *am* worried. Shall we wait and see Uncle Julian?"

"He might be ages yet. If we go straight home we can have a swim before lunch. I want to see if I can beat Pam in the backstroke."

She did. I could race her in the crawl and the breast-stroke but her backstroke was more efficient than mine and she enjoyed giving me tips to improve my style. Wesley sat on a stone bench right by the edge at the deep end and watched us. I asked him why he didn't come in, too, but Charis took my arm and shook her head at me before he muttered, "I don't want to."

"He won't ever come in the pool," she told me when we had swum across to the other side. "He can't swim and he's terrified of water, yet sort of fascinated by it. He'll sit for hours on that seat, watching the light on the surface and the pattern of the tree shadows and the leaves floating and if we're swimming he loves to come and watch. But he had a fright when he was young, at the time of his accident. There was a river. And last year he fell in one night. Dad says we're never to press him to come in the water. We're just to let him look and maybe he'll get over his fear in time."

"Hurry up, you two," called Diella. "It's time for lunch."

I didn't like to ask for more details while Wesley was so close, in case he sensed that we were talking about him. I was becoming very sorry for Wesley.

Vera Elliott, the schoolteacher aunt, called that afternoon. The girls had gone out with friends to a roller skating rink and I was left to my own devices, as I appeared to have no duties other than being a companion to Charis and Diella. Fiona wouldn't even let me help her with the afternoon tea and I found myself alone with Miss Elliott on the terrace. She wore a faded print dress and a misshapen fawn hand-knitted cardigan. Her grey-brown hair, cut short, hung straight, wispy, untidy. But as before, I sensed something straightforward and honest about her. She wasted no time on small talk about the weather. She asked me about my life in England, what schools I'd attended, the job I'd had, whether I had leave of absence from it or would have to go on the dole when I returned, the sports I took part in, my year at Oxford. I felt I was a pupil being assessed for personality and intelligence yet I didn't resent her questions. In fact, I found myself telling her how disappointed I'd been when a reverse in the family finances made it necessary for me to leave Somerville and earn my living. We discussed University life and the advantages of studying the classics.

After a while she frowned—or rather her permanent frown deepened—as she said, "I cannot understand why Max and Fiona went to such considerable expense to bring out an English girl for three months to improve their daughters' manner of speech. It's ridiculous."

She wasn't the first to think that. I couldn't understand either. "Have you asked them?" I enquired.

"Of course I have. I remonstrated when they first told me of the crazy idea. But it's not for me to interfere. Max was the one who proposed it and Fiona had no objection. Well, they can afford it. But Charis and Diella are sensible children. They don't need a nursemaid. Nor is their speech bad and there are plenty of well-qualified elocution teachers in Auckland they could take lessons from if it was considered necessary. There's no harm done, certainly. You have a pleasant voice and an admirably clear way of talking. I was so afraid they'd have chosen someone with that silly vocal affectation which some misguided parents think it a social advantage to adopt. Some of our private schools are adept at endowing their pupils with that particular badge of snobbery."

"Don't Charis and Diella go to a private school?"

"No, they attend the Epsom Girls' Grammar School, which is one of our better state secondaries. In fact, that's why Max moved here. They had a lovely home in Glendowie overlooking the sea and with access to the boat marina. They could have afforded St. Cuthbert's or Diocesan, both excellent private schools, but the Grammar Schools have a particularly fine record of scholastic achievement. They accept only those living within certain limits, so properties in the grammar zone are sought after. That doesn't mean only wealthy families have their children at the school. The zone includes poorer districts, like Grey Lynn and parts of Mt. Eden. So girls from all classes of society will be the constant companions of Charis and Diella. Do Max and Fiona honestly imagine that three months with a well-spoken English young lady in their own home will counteract the effect of daily contact with their school mates? Nonsense."

"I can't see why they wanted someone to come," I admitted, "but I was very lucky to be the one chosen. To find myself in such lovely surroundings with such a super family—it's unbelievable."

She looked at me sharply. "Do you see much of Wesley?"

"He comes with the girls and me sometimes when we drive out. He seems fond of the girls. He sat watching us when we went for a swim in the pool this morning but Charis says he never goes in because he's afraid of water?"

It was a question and she answered it. "He had an unpleasant experience as a child but he wasn't really terrified of water until last year, when there was a bit of skylarking near the pool during a barbecue one evening and Wesley fell in. He can't swim, not a stroke. It was dark, with only the pole lanterns on and others were in the pool, so his shouts were not immediately recognised as cries for help. Fortunately someone swam up to him, saw that he was fully clothed, realised he was in trouble and helped him out. But he had a bad fright, swallowed a lot of water and was hauled out coughing and choking. An unpleasant experience for anyone and his previous fear of drowning was intensified."

"Yet he sat on that bench just near the edge this morning. Isn't he afraid of falling in?"

"No. Why should he be? He's not a complete fool and if he's alone he has no fear of falling. He claims that on the night of the barbecue he was pushed in. He will never sit on that bench if there are others in the garden."

"Pushed? Who do you think pushed him?"

She was silent for a while, frowning and pursing her lips. Then she said, "That is better left unsaid. There was a crowd at the barbecue and too much to drink. Jostling was natural and Wesley was undoubtedly knocked in accidentally while he was standing too near the edge. That is what he believes himself."

I wondered about that. She had just said he claimed he was pushed in. Would he really be so afraid of water or of sitting on the bench with others about if he accepted that it was an accidental knock?

Fiona came out then and I helped her lift the tea trolley over the doorstep on to the terrace. Mrs. Bronson was following her and I offered to fetch Mr. Bronson and Wesley from the garden. Afternoon tea in New Zealand is something like elevenses but at three-thirty or four in the afternoon. I'm used to it now but at that stage it was a novelty.

There was almost no wind, the sky was blue and we sat at tables sheltered by huge sun umbrellas. The surroundings could hardly have been more pleasant and the freshly baked scones with home-made strawberry jam were delicious. I'd have to watch my diet in this household. But tomorrow, not today. Miss Elliott and Mr. Bronson began discussing the latest strike at the Marsden Point oil refinery and the growing antagonism of unions to the government's wage and price freeze. It was interesting to listen to, because although both of them condemned the militant attitude of the union leaders, their suggestions for a method of dealing with it were completely different. Miss Elliott's views were based on theoretical knowledge, those of Mr. Bronson on practical experience in the world of business management, export trade and profit-making. I stretched my legs out into the sunshine and enjoyed the gentle warmth as I listened.

But all the time, at the back of my mind, was the memory of that pill box found in my overnight bag and the knowledge that Mr. Bronson was not wholly convinced that I'd had nothing to do with it. It was not mentioned that afternoon. I knew Miss Elliott had been told about it, as had all the relatives by now, but I had no way of knowing if she considered me involved in the drug trade. Is that why she had questioned me so closely? The thought nagged and nagged and suddenly I had a longing to go home to the fog and the cold and the friendly drenching rain of Richmond, London. How rash I'd been to come! I'd given up my job, too, and as Miss Elliott had suggested, I might have to go on the dole when I returned. Why did I ever see that ad.?

When Miss Elliott left and said goodbye to me, she added, "Take care of yourself, Pamela. Come and see me any time you feel like it. And Mary. Mary's all right. Go round and see Mary. She'll make you welcome." Then, as she was turning away, she murmured quietly, "And meantime . . . watch your step."

5

THUS the days slid by. We went for
a swim in the pool nearly every
morning before breakfast and
sometimes during the day. Fiona seldom
joined us but Wesley liked to come and
watch, acting as judge in any races we had
and laughing happily if one of us ducked
another. The Mirage was at my disposal
to take the girls wherever we wanted to
go. Fiona didn't use it much herself and
Mr. Bronson had his own car, so we went
out frequently. Sometimes we made
longer trips—once to the thermal regions
of Rotorua, staying the night at a motel,
another time to the hot springs at
Waiwera. All expenses were paid by Mr.
Bronson and the amount never questioned. The girls had plans to take me to
some famous caves, to the summit of the
volcano, Rangitoto, to an island off the
coast, and to various beaches which I had

not yet seen. It was as though I were an honoured guest, being shown the sights.

The second time that we went to church the vicar remembered my name and some of the congregation my face, and once more I had pointed out to me the top of Uncle Julian's head. I was becoming known to the man who kept the corner dairy and when the postman stopped me in the next street one day to give me some mail from home, I really felt I was being accepted in the neighbourhood. It should all have been most enjoyable, seeing a new country, living in the luxury of a well-equipped house amid a pleasant, intelligent, hospitable family. The two girls were cheerful, well-behaved, delightful young companions.

But all the time the thought of that heroin in my bag was at the back of my mind, spoiling my enjoyment, refusing to let me relax. I didn't like the way Mr. Bronson looked at me sometimes, as though he wasn't sure I was a fit associate for his daughters after all. They went on a few long day-trips without me, using public transport, and, of course, that was quite natural, considering the difference in our ages, but I had an idea that he arranged those outings. There was no talk of the promised weekend at Waitangi, nor of the yacht trip we had been going to make to some of the islands in the gulf. He twice mentioned the date on which my three months would be up and on the second occasion added that when the school holidays were over there'd not be much point in my staying on, of course he'd pay me the full three months' salary —and the salary was a generous one, more than I'd expected—but we'd see, we'd see . . .

Old Mrs. Bronson didn't talk to me much. When she did she put on that artificial brightness which elderly women sometimes adopt to prove there's life in them yet. It didn't suit her. It was insincere, superficial small talk, twittered in a brisk manner, and didn't fit what Charis had told me about her lively arguments with the vicar. She'd look at me with such keen eyes that I wondered what she really thought. Once she abandoned the "Isn't it a fine day? Do you think we'll get rain tomorrow?" nonsense and began asking me about the detection of drug carrying in England. I was grateful for more gritty conversation with her and started to tell her of a recent case reported in the papers just before I left, when I suddenly realised that she might be pumping me to see how much I knew and that she, too, didn't believe that I'd never seen that heroin before. I closed up then and she nodded, as if to herself, confirming her suspicions. I could almost hear her deciding, "Just as I thought—guilty as hell".

But the two girls remained friendly and natural. There was no suspicion on their part, I was sure of that. They told all their friends and disco and skating companions about the heroin. "It's not *visitors*," explained Diella. "Dad said not *visitors*," and in my ignorance I didn't try to stop them because it was refreshing to have the incident treated as a joke, and after all, it was only what the family thought that mattered to me.

We saw Fiona's sisters several times. The girls liked their aunts and I did, too. I admired Aunt Vera's straightforwardness and the decided, if prejudiced, views she expressed. She was a dedicated teacher, one could see that, and she spoke of her pupils with concern, if not affection. Yet she was looking forward so much to her retirement that I guessed the job was getting her down. She referred once to "the sympathy and tolerance felt towards difficult pupils by those who don't have to teach them". She was said to be a good disciplinarian and I knew from friends at home how much nervous energy must be sacrificed to maintain good discipline in a classroom. She was happy to discuss her future trip to Britain and I invited her to stay with my family. "And us, too, Pammy," said Diella. "We're going to come and stay with you, aren't we?"

"Of course you are," I assured her and she gave me an answering hug.

Mrs. Mersey, their Aunt Mary, was an outgoing, generous woman. Her conversation was not intellectual but it was persistently cheerful and tolerant and her laughter infectious. Only once was her husband Harry home when we called. He was sober this time but I still felt a sort of repugnance. There was something I can't describe, a meanness, a sneakiness. You know? One of those people you instinctively feel would try to keep a railway compartment to themselves by spreading out coat, bag and newspaper to deceive you into thinking all seats were taken. *That* sort of person. He spoke politely on this occasion and said nothing offensive, but I didn't trust him one inch. I didn't know how the girls could be so friendly towards him and I admired their manners and tolerance. One day at the Bronsons' I got the talk on to barbecues and discovered that he and his wife had been present on the evening Wesley fell into the swimming pool. There'd been "too much to drink". Was Harry Mersey the one who had knocked Wesley in? Some silly idea of a joke when he'd boozed all his common sense away? Or a deliberate attempt to frighten Wesley, even perhaps to drown him? I wouldn't have put that past Uncle Harry.

Then one day Fiona's younger brother, Julian, called, the one who played the organ in church and the top of whose head I had been twice ordered to look at. He was thirty-three, they'd told me, had been married in his early twenties and lost his wife to the charms of a Dalmatian. He was divorced now and kept clear of women. He had a long face like his sister Fiona and a pugnacious chin, exuding that type of self-confidence that inspires either dislike or envy. I admire it myself because it's something I know I lack. Anyway, he came to the house one Saturday morning, Charis called me to come and meet him; I looked at him and he looked at me and wham! It happened. In one brief glance, in one second of time, it was like an interchange of philosophies, hopes and innermost thoughts. He wasn't handsome like Talbot but there was fire in his eyes—the real, live fire that Talbot lacked—and he had a kind, expressive mouth. He didn't stay long that first time, he'd just come to bring Wesley a new cassette. But I knew we'd meet again. I'd make sure we did.

There would be plenty of time to see him. My duties continued to be so very light. If I helped with the housework or meal preparations, it was from choice. I was never asked to. Fiona offered me the use of her Mirage even if the girls were out, but I hesitated to use it for mere joyriding. I never ceased to wonder what right I had to be there at all. Mr. Bronson's speech could have passed for that of an educated Englishman. His wife spoke with a New Zealand accent but in such a soft, well-modulated voice that it was not unpleasant. As for the girls themselves, their chatter was full of schoolgirl slang but their diction fairly clear and as Miss Elliott had pointed out, there were plenty of voice production experts they could have been sent to. It seemed amazing to me that I'd been brought all that way, at such expense, because I happened to have spent one year at an

Oxford college and my reading test had pleased a London agent. What could I accomplish in three months? I became over-conscious of my own speech in an effort to earn my wages. I corrected the girls when they lapsed into slovenly expression. I told them how the word "yes" gives away the nationality of a New Zealander in Britain, and they tried to copy the way I said it. The instruction was always good-humoured. They thought it a bit of a joke but they went along with it.

As for being a companion to them, that, too, was nonsense. I was thirteen years older than Charis and both of them regarded me more in the light of a big sister than a comrade. They had accepted me, they liked me, they enjoyed my company in limited amounts, but my advanced age placed me in a world apart. Nor did they need supervision. I met many of their school friends, normal teenagers, some scatty, some serious, some from poor homes, others who had nestled all their lives in opulence and luxury.

There were none whom I considered undesirable company for Charis and Diella.

Nor was there any animosity or jealousy between the two. If they had an occasional disagreement and threw schoolgirl epithets at each other, it was soon over, mainly because of Charis's placid disposition and her willingness to cede a point. They were kind to Wesley and I liked them for that. He came for a short walk with us once and I saw why they did not usually invite him for he walked very slowly, stopping frequently to stare at a tree or examine the shape of a flower hanging over a fence. He still had the child's ability to delight in his surroundings and feel wonder at all he saw. Chief, the dog, would run round him in circles until he was ready to move on again, but we weren't prepared to do that and the waiting was sometimes irritating. When he came in the car with us he was no trouble, sitting quietly in the back seat and hardly speaking. In fact, if the dog came, too, he paid more attention to him than to us. But he usually refused our invitation, preferring to walk alone, sit in the garden or listen to music.

He had his own stereo in his bed-sitting room and used it in preference to the one in the lounge. Julian had helped him set it up and he was immensely proud of it, not allowing anyone else to touch it in case they interfered with the delicate adjustments he'd made. Like many retarded persons he had a certain mechanical ability and Julian had taught him a lot. He kept asking me to listen to his tapes and records and I went in once or twice to please him, when the girls were out. One couldn't help liking Wesley. He was gentle, slow, and anxious to please. You didn't discuss the fourth dimension with him, or the political situation in Afghanistan. But he wasn't an idiot. He'd talk about the plants in the garden, giving botanical names I'd forgotten myself, and he liked to tell me how the spaniel had done something clever, or where one of the neighbours had spent a holiday weekend. There was a complete lack of malice in all his chatter. He was fond of Charis and Diella but seemed particularly devoted to Julian and that to me showed excellent taste.

I considered that Mr. Bronson was unnecessarily impatient with him at times but Fiona explained to me that Wesley was an embarrassment to his brother, whose image with influential associates was important to his business standing in the community. Colleagues who came to dinner or for drinks in the evening did not always understand that Wesley's behaviour was the result of an accident, not congenital idiocy, and in no way reflected on Max's own mental capacity. There had been one or two misunderstandings.

I didn't like to enquire too deeply. It was none of my business. But I noticed that when Wesley was present at a dinner party he was very quiet, speaking only when directly addressed. Was that natural shyness, or was he under orders? Sometimes he was not at the table at all. Confined to his room, so as not to contaminate the intellectual atmosphere? Yet *I* was permitted to be there and I was not capable of intelligently taking part in the discussions which took place on the liquidation of a local finance group or the restructuring of business sectors necessitated by the new trade arrangements with Australia.

Mr. Bronson took me aside one day, just as we were about to go out in the car and were waiting for Wesley, who had decided to come with us.

"Is Wesley behaving?" he asked me.

"Yes, Mr. Bronson. What do you mean?"

"You don't have to take him. It's entirely up to you."

"I don't mind at all. The girls invited him." He talked of poor Wesley being "taken" as though he were an animal.

Mr. Bronson looked a bit worried. "Well, I didn't tell you before. Wesley has . . . let's call it occasional outbursts of temper. It's in no way his fault, you understand. It's a feature of his condition. But stand no nonsense. If there are any

. . . troublesome incidents, tell me at once and I'll see that you aren't bothered again. I don't want you to have any unpleasantness while you're here."

I watched Wesley closely after that. I didn't want any temper tantrums to deal with. But they didn't come. He seemed grateful to be permitted to accompany us, yet rarely agreed to do so. I had the impression that he knew he was an embarrassment, a nuisance, to the family. Fiona showed the most sympathy. "He's very wealthy," she told me. "It's a shame he can't make better use of his money. We've suggested he go on a world trip. He could well afford to pay for a companion to see to formalities at airports and so on. But he's not interested. A pity."

A pity that he could not so conveniently be got rid of? "He seems contented enough," I remarked.

"Yes, perhaps we're wrong to feel sorry for him. He never complains. But one can't discuss it with him. Julian's the closest to him but Julian doesn't often come here. He lives in Ellerslie."

And Ellerslie, I already knew from the girls' geography lessons to me, was not far away. Moreover, Julian owned a car. So why did he not come? He couldn't always be too busy, since he had an able partner. Was Julian the black sheep of the family? Mr. Bronson never spoke of him. Was that because of his divorce? Surely not. It's too common these days. Had he committed some crime in the past? I was intrigued and felt I must find out, kidding myself it was mere curiosity when actually I was just longing to see the fellow again.

Then one day, about two weeks after I'd arrived, a disturbing incident occurred. I was alone in my flat. Mr. Bronson was at work, Wesley out with the dog, the girls with some school friends and Fiona at a bridge afternoon. Old Mrs. Bronson was in her room. She often took a nap in the afternoon.

I was standing with my door open, looking out at the garden, when a man walked round to the back of the house.

He was well-dressed and sleek-haired and widely smiling, giving an instant impression of a salesman or land agent.

"Mrs. Bronson's out," I told him.

"You're Miss Martin?" he asked.

"Yes." I was surprised that he should know my name.

"I've heard about you. News gets around."

"I suppose so." I waited.

"Enjoying your stay in the country?"

"Yes, thank you." What did the fellow want? "Do you want me to tell Mrs. Bronson that you called? If you care to give me your name?"

"No, no. It's you I came to see. Just to let you know . . . I'm in the market."

"Oh? You sell fruit and vegetables? Mrs. Bronson does all the ordering."

He grinned more widely. "Well, you're a cool one, you are. It's all right. You don't need to play the sweet innocent with me. And I pay well. If you've got any more goods, I'll market for you."

"I don't know what you're talking about."

89

"All right, play dumb. But you'll find it hard to get rid of the stuff yourself if you have no contacts. Too risky. Undercover cops all over the place. I'm no cop. You can trust me. I'll give you a good price and no risk. But it's up to you. Think it over. I'll be in touch again."

"Who are you? What do you want? What's your name?"

"Shall we say . . . Smith? But *I'll* contact *you.*" Then he walked away round the side of the house and I heard a car start up in front.

I guess I'm a bit slow at times. It wasn't until after he'd gone that I realised he might be referring to that heroin. He wasn't an addict himself, or he wouldn't have been so casual, but he was offering to sell it for me. So someone on the plane *had* put it into my bag? And informed their contacts in the city? He couldn't know it had been destroyed. Or did he think I had some source of further supplies?

I didn't like to tell the Bronsons. I hoped I'd frozen him off. But two days later I got a phone call. Charis took it and fetched me. The phone was out in the hall. I had a sudden hope that my family were phoning from England to ask how I was or tell me some news. But it was this man again. I knew his voice at once.

"Thought over my little proposition, Miss Martin?"

"I don't know what you want or what you're talking about. Please don't bother me like this."

"You'll find it's not as easy as you think," he said. "You'll need me in the end. Come to your senses, Miss Martin. I'll phone again." Then he hung up.

I put down the receiver and stood for a minute wondering what to do. So he intended to keep on pestering me? He'd phone again. The horrible pseudo-grandfather clock was sneering at me with its wheezy uneven voice as I remained there, confused and upset. "He'll phone again," it seemed to say. "Again, aGAIN, pause . . . again, aGAIN, pause . . ."

I went back into the lounge.

"An admirer?" asked Diella. "Was he inviting you out to dinner?"

"No, certainly not. Mistaken identity. He thought he knew me but he doesn't." I tried to laugh it off but I hadn't liked the tone in that man's voice and the threat to phone again. I wished I had someone to discuss it with. The girls were too young, Mr. Bronson suspicious of me, Fiona too vague. Aunt Vera's knowledge of the world was too restricted, Aunt Mary's sphere was recipes, knitting patterns and garden seeds. There was no one to confide in and consult.

6

WESLEY'S behaviour continued to be polite and friendly towards me but I kept thinking of what his brother had said and was now on my guard in his presence. I knew that the effects of certain forms of mental impairment are unpredictable and can be dangerous. There may be long periods of apparent sanity and then a sudden unexpected outburst of irrational behaviour and even violence. Was that why Vera Elliott had advised me to watch my step?

When she called in one morning I had the opportunity to ask her. The girls were at a jazzercise class, Fiona was visiting a neighbour and Mrs. Bronson senior had taken a walk to the local library. Wesley was in his room playing his records and Miss Elliott did not ask to see him. "Just tell Fiona I was passing by and popped in to say hullo."

"Won't you have a cup of coffee before you go?" I asked, and as she hesitated I added, "I'd love one myself and I have all the materials in my little flat. I'm really spoiled here, you know. Do come and see what luxury I live in."

She smiled at that and accepted. "Yes, it's a nice flat," she said as we sat with our coffee and biscuits at my kitchenette table. "It was built for Max's mother when they first moved here but she had a heart attack once and Fiona thought she could keep a better eye on her if she lived in with the family. They use the flat for visitors, so it isn't wasted, and if they ever sell, it will have added to the value of the property."

"I'm lucky to have it."

She gave me a quick look but said nothing in reply. Then she commented on the pot plant which Fiona had placed on my window sill. It was some time before I could get her off plants, gardens and questions about cultivation in England. In the end I just came out abruptly with the question I was waiting to ask. "Miss

Elliott, why did you tell me the other day to watch my step?"

She looked momentarily embarrassed and then said quickly, "Oh, did I say that? We must all watch our step in these troubled times, mustn't we? I didn't mean . . ." She stopped, waited a few seconds and then resumed her normal, direct manner. "Yes, I *did* mean it, Pamela." She went on thoughtfully, as if choosing her words with care. "You know that I'm a schoolteacher and have been one for many years. We deal with those who are only half-developed in stature, intellect and emotional stability. The study of school children shows up reactions and feelings which are better concealed in their elders but none the less potent."

"You mean it helps you to understand adults? People like Wesley?"

"When a child is deprived of what another has, and knows it—whether it's material goods or success at sport or a handsome face or scholastic ability or whatever—there is sometimes a deep resentment which festers unnoticed. Some accept their lot resignedly, some cheerfully, but in a few a sense of injustice will secretly seethe and expand until it spills over in spiteful acts or even violent ones. Adults react in exactly the same way. Now I would love another cup of coffee, please."

She held out her cup but I wasn't going to let her drop the subject so easily. When I'd poured us both more coffee and come back to the table, I persisted.

"Does Wesley know that he's different from others?"

"Wesley? Why do you ask that? Of course he does. It's very rare for a retarded person to be unaware of his deficiencies."

"Does he mind?"

"Who knows? One hesitates to discuss it with him. I don't see much of him myself. Julian is better able to answer your question."

I hoped then to get her talking about Julian but she looked at her watch, hurriedly drank her coffee and said she must go. I wondered whether to tell her about the man who'd come to see me. I trusted her, as one does tend to trust dowdy schoolmistresses—the training of one's youth, I guess. But she was in a hurry and even if I detained her she might have no useful advice to give. What would a schoolteacher know about the drug world? Besides, I couldn't swear her to secrecy. She would have every right to tell her sisters and I didn't want that. So I walked to the gate with her and said goodbye and yes, I'd certainly drop in one day with the girls. But what she'd said disturbed me and when Wesley came out and asked me to go and hear a record he'd recently bought I made some excuse to go back to my flat.

I like to think that at that stage I had one brief moment of common sense, because I considered going to the police, seeing the two men who had interviewed me and telling them all about it. But then I decided it would only make them more suspicious of me, giving them the idea I was trying to clear myself by implicating one of my colleagues. Besides, I couldn't tell them where to get hold of the man Smith, and he hadn't really said anything incriminating or done anything I could justifiably complain of.

The next day was Saturday and Julian called again. I gathered this was unusual and I was conceited enough to think he might have come to see me. I was certainly glad to see *him*, not only because I was so attracted to him but because I felt he was the one person I could confide in. He knew about the heroin—who didn't?—but I believed he would accept my version of the incident and give me some good advice. I wanted to ask him about Wesley, too. I didn't like to question the others as it might appear that I was criticising poor Wes or commenting rudely on his mental state.

It was some time before I could get Julian alone but he kept looking at me and he wangled it himself in the end. "Do you find our plants out here very different from those at home, Pamela?"

I played along and soon he was taking

me down the garden to see the hibiscus and the native fuchsia. We sat on the padded two-seater lounge swing and ignored the hibiscus and the fuchsia.

"Wesley enjoys this swing," I told him. "He likes me to sit in it while he pushes me and then I swing him in turn."

"Yes, it's one of his favourite spots. He spends a lot of time in the garden, doesn't he? He's quite knowledgeable about plants and he helps Fiona with the weeding."

I didn't hedge. Not with *him*. I got straight to the point. "Julian, does Wesley have a bad temper?"

Julian looked surprised. "I've seen no signs of it."

"Neither have I, but Mr. Bronson says that he has turns now and then, that it's a feature of his condition. As he's so fond of you, I thought you would know."

"He's not an epileptic, I know that, and I've never seen him in a paddy. But something like that could have developed. I don't really see much of Wesley now. I bring him a tape occasionally, that's all.

He used to come to church and enjoy the organ playing. But he hasn't been lately. He gets bored sitting through the liturgy. If he wants to see me he prefers to walk over to my shop in Newmarket and eat my chips, but I bet he doesn't tell his brother that."

"He's not a mongol and you say he's not an epileptic. What's the matter with him, then? I haven't liked to ask the others."

"Oh, didn't they tell you? He had an accident as a small child. The Bronsons used to have a large dairy farm in the Waikato—that's one of the richest farming districts of the country—and they were enormously wealthy. There were just the two sons. Max is the elder by five years. The father took young Wesley out with him on a tractor one day and it overturned. They fell into a river and the tractor only just missed rolling on top of them. Wesley's head was damaged and also he nearly drowned. Whether it was lack of oxygen through half-drowning or the physical damage done by the fall, no one seems to know, but his brain was affected. He's been to specialists. They even took him to America once, but nothing can be done. Certain cells destroyed."

"Oh, poor Wesley."

"I don't know about that," argued Julian. "It seems a pitiable state to us but he may be better off than we realise. Thought never brings happiness, does it? And Wesley always appears content, more so than most people, I'd say. He has loads of money so he doesn't want for anything. His father blamed himself bitterly for the accident and, of course, he *was* to blame. It was madness to let a small child ride a tractor with him on a slope and he knew it. Good lord, the danger is advertised widely and there are often incidents occurring that way reported in the daily newspapers. He never forgave himself. They say that's why he sold the farm and moved into town. He changed his will, too. Gave a life interest in a portion of his assets to his wife, a few hundred thousand to Max and left the bulk of his estate to

Wesley, so that he could at least be properly looked after and need never go into a Home. Until a few years ago he had a flat in Epsom but Fiona offered to let him live with them, so that he wouldn't be lonely. Loneliness is the greatest disadvantage of a condition like his."

"And Fiona brought her mother-in-law in from the granny flat. She's a nice person, Julian."

"One of the best. I'm awfully lucky in my sisters. They're all good sorts."

"But wouldn't Wesley be less lonely in a Home?"

"I've sometimes wondered that. Harry Mersey keeps saying he ought to be put somewhere like that. But it would have to be the right sort of Home. The other inmates in a mental institution would provide no company because he's not an idiot by any means. He's just a little slow. He's actually quite adept at elementary electronics and he knows every wire of every circuit of that stereo of his. Max lets him do any small electrical repairs round the house, too. Yet if he went into some rest home, the others might make fun of him. And an old folks' home wouldn't do either. Actually, I've been looking round for something suitable, and there's one called Fairhaven that doesn't sound too bad. In the meantime Fiona assures me he's no trouble living here. He's another mouth to feed, of course, but he works in the garden, takes the dog for walks and keeps his own room clean and tidy. But you'd better take notice of what Max says. I'm not in a position to know what Wesley is really like these days because I see so little of the family. I'm the other skeleton in their family closet."

"The other? Is poor Wesley regarded in that light?"

"Max isn't too happy about having him in the house. You can see his point of view. He has important business guests and his standing among them means a lot to him. He's a social climber, old Max, and Wes can come out with some inane remarks at times at the dinner table."

103

"And what have you done to be the second skeleton?"

"Nothing criminal or exciting. I've actually led a most uneventful life. Max and his mother just regard me as someone not quite nice to own as a relative because of what I choose to do for a living. Selling fish and chips is vulgar in their eyes and it's not good for Max's status in the business community or at the Grange Golf Club to have me as a brother-in-law. Not at all what he'd have chosen. Oh, we get on all right, but I respect their wishes and keep out of the way most of the time. I have no social ambitions myself. Of course, they recognise me on Sundays. Organists are respectable." He grinned, that delightful, confiding grin that I already loved to watch.

"Why *do* you keep a fish and chip shop? What's the appeal? It sounds hard work and smelly."

"It's both. I didn't exactly pick it out as the ideal life-time career, but a friend of mine was keen on buying the business and asked me to go in with him. Maybe some reaction to the Bronson sense of importance persuaded me, a childish urge to shock them all. If we'd opened a dim-lighted coffee parlour with exorbitant prices and fat profits it would be different. Making money is not only forgiven in the Bronson circles, it's admired. It raises one's status to that of gentleman. You are socially desirable as soon as you successfully and legally rob your fellow man."

"But you make a profit now, don't you? Aren't you a little unkind to call money-making robbery?"

"Yes, we make a profit, of course. That's the aim in any business. But we give good value for money. You must come and try our meat potato patties some time—speciality of the house. Our profits are reasonable, our customers happy and so are we. My partner Jock's a great guy. You must come and meet him."

"And you really like the work?"

"Well . . . it was fun at first and I still enjoy meeting all the customers. We have quite a few regulars. But I admit I'm just a little tired of the smell of oil. And I've made my point. I intend to sell out as soon as Jock finds another suitable partner. Perhaps I'll set up a dining-room then, a working man's restaurant with good food at reasonable prices, no expensive trimmings. What do you think of that?"

"I think it would be a commendable public service. I'd patronise it gladly. But didn't you go to University?"

"What, not you, too?"

"I was just commenting, not criticising."

"Yes, I went to Auckland University. First class honours in History and what can one do with that except teach? Heaven forbid. Look at poor Vera. I did lecture for a while but I chucked it in. Then I worked as a clerk in the Internal Affairs. No, they didn't fire me. I was a jolly good clerk, believe it or not. But I left. I'm spoiled because I have an income of my own, though not quite enough to live on comfortably. I can't afford to be completely at leisure and I've no desire to be. I like trying new things but I do nothing exciting. I'm a most uninteresting person, Pam. I've never even been out of New Zealand. Does that shock you? I've no yearning to see other countries because I'm so content with the one I live in. I lack ambition, Max says, and he's right. Now, tell me all about yourself. What do you do, besides smuggle dangerous drugs in your handbag?"

He was laughing at me and I knew at once that he *did* believe my story. I didn't even comment on that but told him about my own family and my upbringing and my life in England. It was some time afterwards that I mentioned the man who'd come to the house, and the phone call.

He looked serious then. "I don't like that, Pam. The drug world is a very ugly one. There's such enormous profits in the game that all scruples are abandoned and there's fierce competition for any source of supply. He could have been a member of an organised ring. I hope not. Or he could be a free-lance pusher, thinking he'd smelt out a way of making some quick dough. In any case, you be careful."

"How did he know where to find me?"

"Those youngsters Charis and Diella will have told all their mates from school about it, I bet. And they'd pass it on. It must amuse them—a young woman coming out to be a good influence on them and landing next day in the police station, suspected of drug dealing. Even the most respectable of the girls' friends will have relatives, who will have relatives, who will have friends . . . your name and address and the story could eventually be heard by someone to whom it was more than an amusing tale, to be laughed at and then forgotten."

"I've been thinking. Someone on the plane could have got to know my name and address, because of the tag on my overnight bag."

"That's a point. Or even if they didn't know, if they put the stuff in your bag they wouldn't want to lose sight of it. You didn't notice if a car was following you from the airport?"

"No, but I wouldn't have noticed if a fleet of tanks was following me. I was looking at everything in front. It was all so new and exciting. You mean he'd watch to see where I was taken and then come round to see me?"

"Or send someone else. The fellow who came to see you wouldn't be a principal. They keep well screened, often behind legitimate business concerns. I think that man Smith is a small-timer, working on his own."

"What can I do? I tried to make it clear that I wasn't interested but it was no use telling him I didn't bring that heroin in. He wouldn't have believed me."

"I suppose the best thing to do is report the matter to the police. Say you're being pestered."

"But I can't really. I don't know about the rules here, but in England you can't do anything about unwanted phone calls unless they're obscene or threatening.

Besides, the police wouldn't believe anything I said. It would just make them more suspicious of me than ever."

"I see your point. Then I don't know what to advise. I hope the fellow doesn't think you still have the stuff and make an attempt to burgle the place."

"I don't think he would because the girls have spread the story far and wide, as you said, and I bet they didn't leave out the bit about their father burning the box and washing out my bag. They thought that was so funny. I haven't told the family about this man coming round. Do you think I should?"

"No, I don't think so, Pam. You say Max is not convinced you're in the clear. Telling him about this caller could increase his doubts about you and even if he believes that you're not involved voluntarily, you've brought a whiff of the drug world into his respectable home. You might find yourself turned out on your ear. Could you really blame him for a reaction like that? But I wouldn't like it to affect him that way. I happen to want you here."

"And I want to stay." I didn't add "since I've met you" but I don't think I had to. "I told him not to phone again but he said he would."

"Perhaps you've put him off but he may have one more try. And, of course, you know him now and could identify him, so if he finds out he's mistaken about you, it could be dangerous."

"No, he was careful not to say anything to incriminate himself and there was no one else there, so he knows I can't do anything to harm him. He was very cagey in the way he talked. I didn't understand him at the time. I thought he was a door-to-door salesman."

"Yes, he'd be careful what he said and he'll probably let you alone now. But if he doesn't? I wonder what you can do about it? I'm not sufficiently *au fait* with the drug world to give you good advice. I know! Why not go and see old Jarrett, the vicar? He's had a lot to do with drugs and drug addicts, and peddlers, too. He was chaplain at Kingstone for three years and the old boy's done a bit of sleuthing in his day. He uncovered a big drug ring once. He's quite a character."

"I like his sermons. Very much to the point."

"I like him as a man, too. That's why I play the organ for him. I suggest you go and tell him all about it. Shall I come with you? After church tomorrow?"

"No, that wouldn't do, because I'd have to explain to the girls and keep them waiting. I'd rather go one day next week when the girls are out and I can get away without causing comment or saying where I'm going."

"All right. But do go, Pam. The old chap'll probably spout the Bible at you— he does that—but don't be put off by it. He might sound a pompous old goat but he's really very shrewd. I've got to know him fairly well since I've been his organist. I say, we'd better go back to the house, or they'll wonder what I've done with you."

The others didn't take much notice

when we went into the house, with the exception of Diella, who gave a wicked knowing grin. Little devil.

7

I DIDN'T really think seeing the vicar
was a very good idea. I had agreed
only to please Julian. But on the
following Tuesday when the girls were
out I rang up and made an appointment,
then told Fiona I was going to stretch my
legs and walked to St. Bernard's vicarage.

I half expected the old vicar to say "Are
you confirmed?" or "Let us join together
in a short prayer", but he didn't. He
shook my hand and invited me in. Then
he said, "You are the young lady from
England who has attended the morning
service on the last three Sundays with
Charis and Diella Bronson."

"Yes. I've enjoyed it, too," I said truthfully. "Especially last Sunday. There was
such a crowd and they all seemed enthusi-
astic and happy."

"I thought so, too. *They sang praises
with gladness and they bowed their heads*

114

and worshipped. Most of them, that is. Mrs. Canning knitted a few rows of the matinée jacket she's begun for her new grandchild—quite understandably, she is anxious to get it finished. The older Mr. Beeton was studying his *Best Bets* during the Scripture reading, but put it in his pocket in order to take part in the hymn. He has a good, strong voice and may be persuaded to join the choir one day. Yes, on the whole there was noticeable cordiality and willing participation. I am glad you enjoyed it. But you didn't come to talk about our church services. Something is worrying you?"

He was looking at me with remarkably keen grey eyes. I nodded and he said, "Sit down and tell me all about it."

So I did. I just talked and talked while he looked at me and somehow at the end of it I thought he might have believed what I said.

"Let's go through the possibilities," he suggested. "You packed your bag at home, it was taken in your parents' car to Heathrow, and then, apart from passing through the security X-ray, it was in your hands until you boarded the plane."

"Yes, it's light and I carried it myself all the time."

"Do you remember if anyone knocked against you, collided with you?"

"I'm sure no one did."

"And you didn't rest it down at any stage—while kissing your mother goodbye, for instance?"

"No, I'm certain I didn't. It was over my arm with my handbag until I was on the plane and it was zipped right up, except once when I opened it to put in a photo I was given. That took only a few seconds and no one else was near enough to reach the bag."

"You put it at your feet when you were shown your seat on the plane. Did you open it?"

"Not at first. Later I did, to take out my cardigan."

"Did you see any signs of tampering then, any indication that the contents were not exactly as you had packed them?"

"None at all."

"Did you leave it open after you'd taken out your cardigan?"

"I may have. Yes, I think I did."

"How often did you leave your seat before Singapore?"

"Twice, I think."

"You say you had a window seat, in a group of three. To place something in your bag anyone other than your immediate neighbours would have had to lean across two other people or else wait until their seats were vacant."

"They were at times. The woman next to me moved back to get a better view of the film they were showing."

"And in Singapore you left your bag in the plane while you walked round the terminal building for an hour?"

"Yes, but as soon as I was back in the plane I opened it to get out my slippers and there was nothing in it then that wasn't there before."

He shook his head at that. "A small packet could be overlooked."

His questions continued, much the

same in content as those the police had asked me. At last he said, "There is no way of determining how and when the heroin was put in your bag. There was opportunity enough. What I find most puzzling is why it was *left* there. Why was no attempt made to retrieve it? One assumes it was hurriedly hidden in your bag for a good reason—perhaps recognition of an official or a rival on the plane, perhaps to avoid being caught with it in the customs check. But why, *why* was it allowed to remain there? That stuff sells for over seven hundred dollars a gramme. Even the very small portion you were carrying would fetch a high price on the market if it were pure."

I wouldn't have called it a "very small portion" but I didn't interrupt to tell him how it had spilled out of a box and we'd cleaned out my bag. I didn't think the amount mattered much. He went on, "I cannot understand why you were allowed to take your bag away from the airport with the drug still in it."

118

"They couldn't have got it out, could they? I had the bag with me all the time."

He brushed aside this objection. "Of course they could. If they'd wanted it they'd have taken it. A distraction, someone falling against you, a snatch—there are numerous ways to those practised in them. That would have presented no difficulty. Getting through customs with it themselves would have been the problem. A drug courier going through Auckland International airport today runs a greater risk of being caught than he did even a year ago. A special drug check team has been set up and is adept at identifying high-risk passengers. The Department has an "alert list" with information, supplied by the National Drug Intelligence Bureau and international sources, of passengers who should be inspected. There are improved methods, too, of identifying items which could be used for smuggling drugs. A high degree of success has been achieved. One can understand a courier hastily getting rid of his packet if he feared detection. But you had passed through customs without being challenged. Why would such a valuable commodity suddenly be sacrificed?"

"But the man who came round that day —didn't he come to collect it?"

"No. If he thought you were still in possession of it, he'd have forced an entry and searched. He knew it had been disposed of but he hoped you were a source of further supply. I don't think he has any connection with those who planted it on you. Another possibility is that he was an undercover policeman."

"Oh! But he told me he wasn't anything to do with the police. He stressed that."

"Just as an undercover man might do. The police engaged in that dangerous work must win the confidence of their quarry before they pounce on him."

"I didn't think of his being a policeman. Do you mean they didn't believe a word I said at the station?"

"It's possible. Fortunately I have contacts at police headquarters whom I can ask."

"But *you* believe me, don't you? That I didn't know it was there? That I'd never seen it before?"

"I'm inclined to believe you but I can't say categorically that I do. You're a well-spoken, open-faced young woman. I've known an equally ingenuous-looking one who is now serving a three-year term for fraud. Don't look so depressed." He smiled. "My professional contacts have made me unwilling to pronounce anyone innocent without proof. I want to believe you. I tend to believe you. But I can't affirm that I do, when I recognise the possibility that you are a member of an international drug gang. I'd certainly like to help you show that you're not."

"Oh dear, what should I do?"

"Return to England as fast as you can."

"But I haven't done anything criminal. Why should I run away?"

"For two good reasons. Firstly, you are now listed on our police records as having been found in possession of a dangerous drug. There will be a file with your name on it, and the facts may also be recorded permanently in the data held by the Wanganui computer. Secondly, you are suspected by at least one man of having a source of supply. Any contact with even a lone peddler on the outside edge of a drug ring puts you at risk. There are times when the wisest course is to run. This is one of them. Run now. Back to your country and your family, preferably by the next plane."

"That's impossible. I've promised to stay three months and then they pay my fare back. Even if I wanted to go now I couldn't buy a ticket."

"You told me that Mr. Bronson suggested you go early. And you could cable your family for the fare, if Bronson was unwilling to pay it."

I could, too. I knew that. They'd have sent it like a shot. I didn't like to tell the vicar about Julian. If I left Julian now he might forget all about me. I couldn't bear that. So I argued weakly, "I wouldn't want to leave the girls."

"Nonsense. They can do without you. Why are you reluctant to go home?

What's the real reason? Have you quar-relled with your family? Did you run away?"

"No, I did not," I said indignantly. "I write to them every other day and I get lots of letters from them."

"I'm glad to hear it. *As cold waters to a thirsty soul, so is good news from a far country*. If it's not a disagreement with your family, what is it that makes you so unwilling to leave? Or *who* is it?" There was a twinkle in his eye as he continued, "My organist, by any chance?"

"Of course not! How could *he* have anything to do with it? I've only just met him." But I couldn't keep it up under that steady penetrating gaze. I capitu-lated. "Oh well, I *would* like to know him better, but he hasn't—we don't—I wasn't —how did *you* know, anyway?"

He grinned at me. "*A thing was secretly brought to me and mine ear received a little thereof.*"

"Those girls! Diella, I bet."

"Don't blame her entirely. One or two remarks Julian has passed also led me to believe that there is a mutual attraction. Is that the case?"

In for a penny, in for a pound. I'd told him so much about myself already that there was no point in holding back. There's something about that old vicar that makes you want to come clean. "I don't know, Mr. Jarrett," I confessed. "I honestly don't know. I like him an awful lot but he's not really my type. He seems to lead such a dreary uninteresting life. I want to *do* things. He could be too dull a person for me."

"Don't be deceived," said the vicar. "People who are in themselves interesting do not need an adventurous life to stimulate their personality. They can be alive and exciting over a pan of sizzling meat patties. As far as I know, Julian has travelled no further than the South Island, he's never shone at sport, he does not speculate or gamble. Apart from one unhappy marriage his life has been devoid of major events. His daily routine is noticeably lacking in thrills and variety, according to you. But he has intelligence and vitality. Does it not occur to you that he may consider it a fascinating adventure to dip a potato chip into a vat of bubbling oil?"

"If you put it that way . . .."

"Others, to whom life offers a wide variety of her entertainments, who travel and indulge in unusual projects or occupations, sometimes learn little in the process and develop only slowly. Have you not noticed that? It may be a stoic or phlegmatic acceptance of all that comes their way, but more likely they are cursed with an impervious wooden husk over a soul of damp cotton wool."

"I see what you mean. Like Talbot."

"Who is Talbot?"

"A man I am *not* going to marry. He lives in England. He's awfully wealthy, he's travelled all over Europe and the States, he won the Southern open tennis singles one year, he once went on a photographic safari in Africa and . . . and I took this job to get away from him. He's so *dull!*"

"Exactly. I would not presume to

dictate to you in the matter of your own feelings, but I do assure you that Julian Elliott has been my organist for several months now and during that time I have found him to be far from dull."

"It's such a funny job to choose—frying fish."

"Do you think so? Which do you consider the better occupation—to keep a small smelly fish and chip bar in Newmarket, with modest profits, or to organise large business concerns which roll remorselessly over all the struggling little corner shops?" I wondered if he was referring to Mr. Bronson. He continued, "I have patronised his shop. He gives good value. *A false balance is an abomination to the Lord but a just weight is his delight*. Julian's customers respect and like him. No doubt you have consulted him over your problem. Did he suggest you go home?"

"He suggested I see you."

"To seek my advice? You know now what that is. If there is any true feeling between you and Julian your going back to England will not destroy it. Go home, Pamela. It's the wisest thing to do."

I thanked him for his advice and he knew jolly well that I didn't intend to take it. He looked troubled as he showed me to the door. "Let me know any further developments," he said, "and don't hesitate to telephone or come to see me at any time if you think I can help."

I walked back. It was only about two miles and yet I felt exhausted when I arrived at the Bronson house. Mental turmoil can be physically tiring.

I freshened myself up and then went into the lounge. As I passed through the hall that wretched clock echoed the vicar's words. "Go back where you belong," it sneered, "back, ger-BACK, pause. . . back, ger-BACK, pause . . . back, ger-BACK . . ."

Old Mrs. Bronson was alone in the lounge, knitting. "None of the others are home yet," she said. "Sit down. Where have you been?"

"For a walk."

"Huh. You be careful, young woman. I think you should go home, back to your own country."

Why did they all want to get rid of me? I had felt so welcome when I first arrived. "I know I'm not doing much," I began in protest.

"Rubbish! You're a great asset to those two girls. They're fond of you and you have a good influence over them. I listen and I watch and I notice what goes on. But I advise you to go home for your own sake. I'm the mother, remember. I know. Go home, my child. Go home while you can."

"Does Wesley know about his accident?"

"Of course he does. He knows he was normal before it happened. But one cannot always . . ."

Then the back door opened loudly, the two girls came into the lounge. "Hullo, Gran. Pam, you should have come to the disco," said Diella. "It was smashing. Did they have discos when *you* were young? What about a swim? Race you to

128

see who gets changed first. Come on, Pammy." She took me by the arm and pulled me out.

8

"CAN I come back to England with you?" asked Wesley.

It was Wednesday morning. The girls had gone out with their friends, Fiona was baking and the cleaning woman had arrived to wash windows under Mrs. Bronson's direction. I had wandered down the garden, where Wesley was sitting beside the swimming pool, the spaniel at his side. The two looked rather alike.

I sat down beside him, a little surprised at the sudden request and wondering how to answer it.

"I'd behave very well," said Wesley.

"Of course you would. You always do. I know that, but it would be difficult," I explained. "There'd be nowhere for you to live over there and nothing for you to do."

"I'd find plenty to do. I'd walk about

130

and look at things and I'd take my stereo."

"The climate is terrible in winter, Wesley, and it will still be winter when I return. You wouldn't like it. And you'd miss all your family. You'd be lonely."

"I could live with your family until I found a flat. I heard you tell Charis that there's plenty of room."

"But they are girls. They would share my room." A downright lie. We had a four-bedroom house.

"I wouldn't be a nuisance. Fiona says I'm never a nuisance. Max thinks I am. Max doesn't like me. But Fiona is kind. And I have a lot of money, they say. I don't need to work and if you didn't have room I could stay in a hotel near you. There's enough money. Lots of it. I don't carry it with me, they don't let me, but all I have to do is ask the lawyer, he's very kind too, and if I want any-thing . . ."

"Look, Wesley, you couldn't come back with me. There are immigration restrictions." He looked puzzled. "They don't just let people come into the country and settle there. Besides, you wouldn't want to leave the girls, would you? Or Julian?"

His face fell. "You don't want me to come with you? I'm not a nuisance. Fiona says I'm no trouble. I clean my own room and I don't ask for things."

"It's not that I wouldn't want you there, Wesley." Another lie. Being sorry for a person doesn't mean that you're willing to take on responsibility for his welfare or have him under your feet all the time. I was selfish, I knew, but I did *not* want him living in England with us or near us. "Perhaps later, for a visit. Say for three months? My family and I would look after you while you were there." We would. We'd give him a really good time and show him the sights. I'd see to that. But for a visit, not permanent residence.

"I'd get all messed up at the airport, they say, I wouldn't know what to do, because I don't think very fast."

"You could afford to pay someone to travel with you, couldn't you?"

"I suppose so. But I'd rather come with you. You don't want me. No one wants me."

"You're wanted here, Wesley. The girls couldn't do without you. Nor could Chief." I patted the dog at his feet and Chief obligingly wriggled an acknowledgment. Then I changed the subject. "Tell me what records and cassettes you've bought recently."

Wesley gradually cheered up. He had bought the latest James Galway flute selections. Then he talked about the flautists in the New Zealand symphony orchestra, naming some of them and giving his preference. I was surprised at his knowledge and encouraged him to talk for some time on musical matters before I went inside again. He seemed happy when I left him. But I remained a little disturbed at his request. I'd thought him content in his life here. How little one really knows about another person's emotions, frustrations and hopes! I'd taken scant heed of what Mr. Bronson had said and he was the one who would know Wesley best.

The next morning the girls were again out by themselves, each with fellow pupils. (What *was* I there for? No one seemed to care what I did.) I went out of my way to find Wesley and talk to him, in order to reassure him that I was a friend.

He appeared to have forgotten the conversation of the day before. "I'll swing you," he suggested.

"All right." We walked down to the bottom of the garden and I sat on the cushions of the lounge swing while Wesley pushed. It didn't swing very high. It wasn't designed for that sort of movement and I hoped that Fiona or Mr. Bronson wouldn't notice our abuse of it. Wesley liked swinging to the limit and I saw no harm in it. If we damaged the swing they could well afford another. It would be my turn to push soon. He preferred me to go first because he then had a longer spell in it himself. He had reasoned that out, so he wasn't too dull.

He was pushing me as high as the

swing would go and I heard his quiet, pleased laugh. Obviously he was enjoying himself and if he did remember yesterday he must have forgiven me for rebuffing him. Then suddenly I was hurtling crookedly through the air. I grabbed at one side rope—the other had gone—hung for a second, then that rope, too, broke under my weight and I landed heavily, clumsily, on a Chinese hollygrape bush. I cursed that prickly bush at the time but it broke my fall. I got up slowly, tried my legs and they worked. I had bruised and scratched myself and my shoulder hurt, but the damage was slight. Then I looked at Wesley. He had the strangest expression on his face. Was it disappointment? Had he been glad when I fell? He hadn't run to help me up. He'd just stood there, unmoving.

"You all right?" he said now, still with that expression of . . . what was it?

"Yes, I'm all right, Wesley, but I'll have to go inside and change." I showed him the soil on my dress.

"You're going to tell *them?*"

"Of course we'll have to tell them. The swing is broken. It must be reported so that it can be mended."

"*You* tell them, please?" He looked normal again, his old self, the gentle, tail-wagging Wesley.

I left him there and walked up to the house, feeling a little shaken. I showered and changed before I went into the kitchen and told Fiona what had happened.

"Oh dear, are you hurt?" she said anxiously. "Just look at those scratches."

I wasn't hurt really. I was just bruised and a bit frightened. I told her so and asked what I could do to help her.

"Well, if you really want to—if you're quite sure you're not hurt and you don't mind—would you care to take some of these small cakes round to Vera? She doesn't bake much herself and she does like these coconut ones. Only if you feel like it," she went on earnestly. "It's not an order, you know."

I didn't stop to point out that I was engaged on a generous salary and was there to take orders. I'd tried that before and it didn't get me anywhere. Instead I said, "I'd love to, Fiona."

"Are you sure you're not hurt? Are you quite fit to go? You must take the Mirage."

"No, thank you. I'll enjoy the walk and I'd like to see your sister again."

'Then would it be too much to ask you to pop this knitting book into Mary as well? If she's not home you could just leave it in the letter box." Letter boxes and milk boxes in New Zealand are erected out by the street, usually attached to a gate post or the front fence. I thought it primitive at first but it has its advantages.

"Of course." I was glad to get away from the house, alone. Wesley's attitude worried me and if it hadn't been for Julian I think I would have considered the vicar's advice right then and thought about going home.

I was wearing a short-sleeved dress, so both the bruise on my forehead and the scratches on my arms were obvious.

"What *have* you done?" exclaimed Vera Elliott.

"I just had a fall."

But you don't get away with a vague answer like that to Vera. I soon found myself describing the accident and she questioned me closely. *"Both* ropes? How very strange. It shouldn't give way like that. They bought it from the Farmers Trading Company not very long ago. A most reputable firm. Max must take it back and complain. Are you sure you're not badly hurt? You didn't land on the concrete?"

"No, I landed with my head on soft soil and my body in a Chinese hollygrape."

"Oh dear, did you break it?"

It was the bush she meant, not my body. I assured her it would survive the blow and left before she could question me further, on the excuse of having to take a pattern to Mrs. Mersey before lunch.

There was no answer to the front door bell at the Merseys' house so I strolled round the back. Harry Mersey was sitting outside in the sun and saw me before I could retreat.

"Good morning," I said coldly. "Is Mrs. Mersey home? I have a pattern book for her from Mrs. Bronson."

"The wife's out. Won't be home till lunchtime. I'll give it to her. Sit down for a minute, girl. You look washed out." He indicated another chair.

At least he was not drunk and because I was tired—the fall had shaken me up more than I realised at the time—and because I didn't like him and was ashamed of it, I sat down.

"What the hell have you done to yourself?"

"I fell over just before I came out."

"Fell? You wouldn't be stinko at this hour of the morning."

I forbore to point out that there are causes of falling other than the one with which he would be most familiar.

"Sit there, girl. I'll get some coffee."

I let him. I didn't even protest. What I wanted most of all at that moment was a cup of strong coffee and I didn't care who dispensed it. I just sat and rested in that cane chair in the sunshine and listened to him rattling cups in the kitchen. He came back before long with two large steaming mugs. "Wait a mo. Get the sugar." He placed the mugs on a table beside us and returned next time with sugar bowl, half a bottle of cream and biscuits in a tin. "Now, what happened? Howja fall?"

I told him. What else could I do? He'd find out later if I didn't tell him now. He looked just as puzzled as Miss Elliott had and said, "*I* helped to put that swing up. Brand-new it was. Straight from the shop. Lemme see . . . October . . . 'bout nine weeks ago it'd be. You want something on those scratches?"

"No, thank you. They're not deep. I landed on a Chinese hollygrape."

"That's a prickly bugger, eh? Made a real mess of you." Then he went on drinking his coffee and said nothing for a while. I decided to make polite conversation. I owed him a little courtesy if only for the coffee.

"I was surprised to find you home, Mr. Mersey. I had imagined your business would occupy you all day."

"Harry's the name, girl. I got a good crew at the yard. Real decent jokers. They run the outfit. I can take a few hours off when I feel like it. When are they going to put that fellow in a Home?"

"What fellow?" But I knew whom he meant.

"Wesley. Flaming ridiculous to keep him with them. Should be put out of harm's way. More coffee?"

"No, thank you." I was annoyed at his last remarks and all my dislike for him came flooding back. "I must go now. Charis and Diella will be home soon."

"The kids don't need you. Sure you're OK to be off? Drive you home, eh?"

"No, thank you. I'm fine and I like walking."

He stood and watched me as I got up. "You be careful, girl. That fellow ought to be in a Home." Then he came round to the front of the house with me and watched as I walked down the street. I know he did because I was silly enough to look round once and was forced to exchange a wave before I turned the corner.

Both his and Miss Elliott's comments prepared me somewhat for what happened that evening. I'd almost forgotten the incident by then. The girls and I had driven out to Piha Beach to see the finals of a surf life-saving contest. We were now having a quick game of Scrabble before dinner.

Mr. Bronson came up to us. "Miss Martin, would you come with me for a minute, please? I shan't keep you long."

"Yes, take her away, Dad," said Diella. "It'll give me more time to make a word out of these perfectly foul letters. I'll sneak a look at the dictionary while she's gone."

He laughed. "Come on then, Miss Martin." He still called me that and I always addressed him as "Mr. Bronson". I didn't know whose place it was to suggest less formality and as I didn't see much of him it didn't really matter. I would have hated to call Fiona "Mrs. Bronson" now, because I was growing to like her more all the time. Her seemingly vague manner concealed a very kind heart. Wesley must have been a bit of a trial to have all the time in her own home but she never complained. It was the same with her mother-in-law, an extra person making more work and restricting her privacy and leisure time. Yet never, in all the time I'd been there, had I heard her utter one word of criticism of either of them.

Mr. Bronson led me down the garden to the swing. "Look." He held out the rope ends and I saw what he meant.

"They're not frayed," I remarked.

"No. They've been cut through down to the last strands."

"But who . . . what . . . ?"

"I don't think we'll say anything about it to the others," he said with a worried frown. "Have you recently . . . annoyed Wesley at all?"

I hesitated. I didn't want to tell him about Wesley's request.

"Well, no matter," he went on. "But do please remember what I told you the other day. My brother is not entirely responsible for his actions. He doesn't reason as a normal person would. He is like a child in many ways and can react in a childish manner. We can't blame him for it. But I must apologise to you for what happened and I'm very glad indeed that you were not seriously hurt. You will be more careful in future?"

I nodded. "Yes, I shall." I meant it. I'd watch myself carefully. Poor Wesley. He was hitting back in a way he could understand. Instead of being angry I felt desperately sorry for him. But I must take care not to offend him any more. I hoped there would be no reprisals against him, no disciplinary measures. It was all very well for Mr. Bronson to say we'd keep it to ourselves. How was he going to explain not returning the swing to the Farmers'? And he wouldn't fool Miss Elliott or Harry Mersey into believing there was any natural cause for both those ropes giving way at once.

After dinner there was another phone call for me. "Miss Martin, this is the businessman who called. Have you any goods you would like me to sell for you? Anything you brought from overseas and feel you have no use for in this land of sunshine? Is there. . . ?"

I slammed the receiver down.

"Your admirer again?" enquired Diella.

I didn't answer. I didn't have time.

"Don't ask questions like that, Diella," said her father sharply. "Miss Martin's affairs are nothing to do with you." I didn't like that word "affairs". What did he think was going on? I was very tempted at that moment to tell them all about it, but Julian had advised against that and what Julian said mattered.

"Do you want me again this evening, girls?" I asked. "I'd like an early night."

"Of course," said Fiona quickly. "You must be shaken after that fall. Can I make you a hot drink before you go? Or bring one in to you? Milo? Horlicks?"

"No, thank you, Fiona. I'd just like to

crawl into bed. I'll be right in the morning."

"Well, stay in bed if you're not."

"Yes, we'll bring your breakfast in," said Charis.

"And we'll come and have ours with you, Pammy," added Diella.

They all said good-night—oh, so nicely. Even Mrs. Bronson senior looked more kindly at me than usual as I left the room. It was only that loathsome grandfather clock that jeered as I passed through the hall. "You fell, ger-FELL, pause . . . fell, ger-FELL, pause . . . fell, ger-FELL . . ." One day, I promised it bitterly, I shall take a clawhammer and smash your silly face to smithereens.

9

THE next day, Friday, the girls and I began our Christmas shopping. The newspaper advertisements had been screaming, ever since I arrived, that there were only twenty more shopping days to Christmas . . . sixteen . . . ten . . . Now there were eight. It didn't feel like Christmas to me. The temperature was in the high seventies most days, the long school summer holidays were in full swing and many families in the neighbourhood had already left on camping or yachting trips.

But English traditions die hard. It amused me to see the shop windows dotted with patches of cotton wool to simulate snow, the card and calendar scenes of sleighs and white fields, and the poor Father Christmases employed by department stores, sweltering under their thick red costumes and black boots and woollen beards.

"That's nothing," said Fiona. "Wait until Christmas dinner, when we have roast turkey, mince pies, plum pudding and hot brandy sauce, all eaten in the middle of the day while the sun streams through the windows. Only the daringly unconventional settle for ham and salad. We even put artificial holly berries on our pudding and hang up plastic mistletoe. We do spare you the yule log, though, and we serve chilled drinks before dinner."

"You'll find it different," said Diella, "but it's just as much fun. We have a Christmas tree and we decorate the lounge. Time we got busy on that, Charis! And our aunts and Julian come to us for the midday meal. We open our presents before we start."

"Which cost no more than two dollars each," Charis told me, "and that applies to you, too, Pam. None of us is allowed to spend more than two dollars on a present for anyone else. It's a strict rule

Dad and Mum made a few years back so that we wouldn't waste money on things they didn't want. Do you think it's silly?"

"I think it's an excellent idea." The Bronsons wanted for nothing and if the girls expressed a wish for some article at any time of the year it would not be a shortage of funds that prevented its being granted.

"It's getting harder each year," said Charis, "with inflation so high. We have to go round the bargain shops or look in oddment trays or make things."

"Are second-hand articles allowed?"

"Of course, or home-made or 'soiled and damaged no refund or exchange'. Anything's allowed as long as it doesn't cost more than two dollars. We've had some fantastic bargains in the past. Remember that flask top you decorated with little transfers, Diella, and gave to Aunt Vera as an eggcup?"

"But the egg rolled round the bottom, didn't it? She used it as a vase for a while. She's a good sport."

"What about the wooden plate you

149

picked up and tried to make a jigsaw puzzle of?"

"I *did* make a jigsaw puzzle. It's just that the saw I borrowed from Jenny's brother was a bit too thick. Remember the rubber elephant Aunt Mary gave you? She said she found it in auction rooms but I think she cheated over that one."

"Yes, that was neat but Chief stole it."

"Oh well, he enjoyed it. Chewed it to bits. Christmas *is* fun, Pam. Let's go to Otahuhu today. There's lots of second-hand shops and surplus army stores there. Though, I think I might *make* some of my presents this year. I've had a fabulous idea of what to do for Pammy."

"Not another book cover, I hope?"

As Fiona was going to bridge in her car, we took the bus. It was fairly full but there were still a few seats. But as we got in, I had a shock. Half-way down the bus, I saw *him*, the man who called himself Smith. I sat down quickly, as I didn't want him to see me. I would have liked to get out at the next stop but couldn't think of any good reason to explain to the girls why we should do so. By the time we reached the town centre at Otahuhu the bus was crowded, with people standing in the aisle. "We get out here," said Charis, and I was obliged to stand and turn towards the rear exit door. I saw he was standing, too, fortunately with his back to me. He was carrying a black attaché case, like those lawyers have. He stood back for some women to go before him and put his case down at his feet. There was some delay. I noticed there was an exactly similar case beside it, belonging, I guessed, to a man still seated. They're a common enough type— the executive's badge of office, the same as in England.

But then, when it was his turn to get out, he reached down and picked up the wrong case. No mistake about it. They were side by side and he took the other man's case. I had a moment of really spiteful satisfaction, hoping he'd lose all his important letters and files or whatever he was carrying around. Then I felt ashamed of myself. I really ought to tell him. But because we were at the front of the bus, and there were so many on that they were enforcing the "rear door exit only", I couldn't see him when we were finally out on the pavement, and that was all the excuse I needed to put any kindly thoughts of helping him aside. I realised it would have been more sensible to point out the mistake to the man still on the bus, but I hadn't thought of that at the time, and it was moving on now.

All right, I'm a bone-headed nit-wit, I know. I suspected the fellow of peddling drugs and it isn't as if I hadn't *read* about stolen goods and fences and drug distribution and so on. But you don't expect it to take place under your very nose. I honestly thought he'd taken that other case by mistake. I brushed off any sense of responsibility. He'd contact the bus company and so would the other man and they'd each get their own property back.

We were in a bustling, noisy street of gaily decorated shops. The footpaths were crowded with shoppers. We kept agreeing to separate, meeting again in ten minutes or so, and then decided to give ourselves a full hour alone, meeting back at a coffee bar for lunch. I wandered from shop to shop, found two broken strings of beads, 95 cents and 60 cents. A new clasp would bring the cost to just the right amount and I could combine the best beads into an attractive necklace for Charis. I was proud of my purchase. Later I found a squashed, but intact, box of raisins and nuts in the Bargain Bin of a grocer's shop. That would do for one of the adults.

I passed through an arcade and made for an auctioneer's rooms which I saw not too far away. There was nothing suitable there and no other shops in the area so I turned a corner to return to the busier part. The street was being redeveloped by the look of it. There were some buildings half-demolished, others in various stages of construction, here and there a small, empty shop. I was half-way down the street when suddenly *he* appeared at the other end. The man Smith. I turned, hoping to reach a corner before he could see me. But there were very few people in the street and he'd probably recognise me from the back. I didn't want him chasing after me and pestering me again, so I hurried a few yards on to the one established building I'd noticed, the Sureway Insurance Company. I could hide in there until he'd passed. I stood in the foyer, congratulating myself on a lucky escape, when I saw his figure through the glass doors, about to come in. He was still carrying the black attaché case. Fool that I was, I should have realised that it was the only building in the street that a businessman would be making for, and he obviously *was* a businessman, peddling drugs on the side. I turned and ran up the stairs. There were only two storeys but there were offices on the upper floor, so I walked hastily along a corridor, choosing one to hide in. *Puffs and Poppers, Children's Parties*. I couldn't see *him* interested in a children's party, so I pushed open the door.

The room smelt of fresh paint. "Do excuse the mess," said a sweet young thing behind a counter. "We just moved in yesterday when the premises became vacant . . . No, we don't organise the party but we do all the catering and the table-setting . . . Yes, all the food is home-made . . . balloons, crackers, that sort of thing on the tables . . . of course, any number . . . certainly, health foods if requested. Has your niece some problem with diet? Diabetes? Oh dear, what a shame, but I'm sure we can organise suitable dishes, looking attractive . . . I see your point. It *would* be upsetting for the little girl to see her guests eating meringues and sweets . . . the middle of March? I'll just take down the particulars and . . . oh, very well, if you prefer to talk it over with the mother first. You can assure her she will be satisfied. We do a good job. Here's our card. The phone will be connected some time today . . . no, we don't have photographs of the settings but . . . yes, of course you must. I understand . . . not at all, that's what I'm here for . . ."

I could prolong it no further and he would surely be out of sight by now. I cautiously opened the door of *Puffs and Poppers*, saw no one in the corridor and walked quietly along the carpeted floor. I had almost reached the stairway when the door of *Moreton Associates* opened and —of all the rotten bad luck!—*he* came out. I was well and truly caught.

He stepped in front of me. "What are you doing here?" he asked sharply. This was an odd thing to say. It was a public building, wasn't it? "Have you something to say to me?"

"Of course I haven't," I replied. "I didn't know you worked here." I glanced through the glass panel on the door of *Moreton Associates* and saw another man standing at a table, a plump swarthy chap with a scar on one cheek. He saw me looking and moved quickly out of sight. Self-conscious about that very ugly scar, I supposed. I went on, "I was consulting the *Puffs and Poppers* girl. My small niece . . ." I stopped in time. He knew I'd just come from England and probably had no relatives here. "I mean my hostess's niece . . ." I stopped again. I owed him no explanation. It had nothing to do with him.

He sneered. "Don't give me that gaff about a niece. The *Puffs and Poppers* outfit have just moved here and haven't advertised their whereabouts yet."

"I came to pay an account at the Sureway Insurance, and . . ."

"Which is on the ground floor," he broke in, "clearly labelled. So you want to talk business, eh? I told you I'd get in touch with *you*. You had no right to come here. Who told you where to come? Who was it? Tell me."

"No one told me you were here. I didn't know you worked in this building and I certainly have no business with you."

"You haven't, eh? Then what are you after? Why are you poking around? Do you know what happens to snoopers in our game?"

I thought fast. It would be better to placate rather than antagonise him and at least I had a reason to trot out. "I was not snooping, Mr. Smith," I said coldly and firmly. "I was in the Sureway Insurance and happened to see you pass through the foyer and up the stairs. I thought it would be only common courtesy to let you know that you picked up the wrong attaché case on the bus. I was travelling on the same one but you had gone by the time I got out."

He was staring at me. I continued, "Naturally I did not know where you work. I came upstairs to find you, saw the *Puffs and Poppers* notice and took the opportunity of making some enquiries about a birthday party coming up. My presence in this building has nothing to do with you and you have no right to speak to me like that."

He was still staring. It was hard to tell if he'd swallowed my story or not. He said slowly, "So I picked up the wrong case, did I?"

"Yes, they looked exactly alike. I thought you'd like to know. Now I'm sorry I bothered."

"I do beg your pardon, Miss Martin," he said with his best salesman smile now.

"I'm certainly grateful to be told. I may not have discovered my mistake for some time otherwise. Oh dear, what a nuisance! I wonder how I can get my own back. You didn't happen to know the man whose case I took, I suppose?" He was all politeness now.

"No, I'm sorry, I'd never seen him before. But I'm sure I'd recognise him again if I saw him, so if I . . ."

"You would?" he interrupted quickly, looking at me keenly.

"Yes, I have a good memory for faces and I'd know him anywhere, so if I pass him in the street—I've got some more shopping to do—I'll let him know where to find you. But you could contact the bus company, Mr. Smith. He may have put your case in at the Left Luggage."

"Yes, yes, of course. I'll do that. Thank you for letting me know, Miss Martin. I'm sorry I spoke as I did. The pressure of business, you know . . . You *are* quite sure you'd recognise this man again?"

"Absolutely," said that green, inane,

unsophisticated muggins, ME. Then I bade him a pleasant goodbye and walked down the stairs, very uncomfortable about the whole conversation. I hadn't liked the look he'd given me or that horrible remark about snoopers. But I'd made an honest account of seeing him take the wrong case and he'd find out that was true when he opened it. So I had nothing to worry about. Or had I?

I tried to be normal with the girls as we had lunch and then did more shopping. They were in a happy mood and had bought a big bagful of decorations and tinsel for the Christmas tree.

They went out after dinner that evening to a friend's place. Their parents were visiting, too, and had taken Mrs. Bronson with them. I was free to do as I pleased. "That wildlife programme you enjoy so much is on at 9 o'clock," Fiona reminded me. "Don't forget to watch it."

"I certainly shan't. Is Wesley going with you?"

"No, he wouldn't enjoy it. He'll spend the evening with that stereo of his. But he's going to put a new plug on the television flex for you first. The one on it is cracked, we noticed."

So Wesley was being left behind, as usual. He must sense that he was unwanted. Yet he gave no sign of it. When they had all left he came into the lounge and looked cheerful as he renewed the plug. He always seemed pleased when he was entrusted with such jobs. As he worked he told me about a new cassette he'd bought that afternoon, a selection of arias from *La Bohème*. "I don't like opera very much but Mr. Davidson— that's the man in the music shop—he said I'd like this one because they're all well-known tunes I'll have heard before and he knows what I like. He's very kind to me. I'm going to go and play it as soon as I've done this. There, that's finished."

He carefully gathered up the scraps of flex and left the room. Soon I heard his stereo playing. He hadn't invited me to hear his new tape and that was unusual. Was he still nursing a grudge against me?

I read for a while but as it neared nine

161

o'clock I got up to turn the television on for the wildlife programme. The set was positioned the other side of the room from the wall socket and one connected it by means of an extension cord which lay along one wall. One day they would have another wall socket put in, Fiona had told me, but it was such a small job that it had been continually deferred. The extension cord was always left plugged in so all one had to do was connect the two cords. They were normally left apart as the extension was also used for the vacuum cleaner, the stereo and a small fan. It was a matter of courtesy to disconnect them after use, for the next person who wanted to use the extension.

I bent down and pushed one plug into the other. There was a sharp crack, a blue flash and a wisp of smoke. I jumped back in alarm. Wesley came in, having heard the noise. He stared at me, then at the plug, and again I saw that peculiar expression on his face.

"You didn't get hurt," he observed. Was there disappointment in his tone?

I walked over to the wall socket and pulled out the extension cord. Then I went back and picked up the two connecting fixtures. Both were blackened. Wesley hurriedly took them from me, saying "I'll fix it", then pulled them apart and started dismantling them with the small screwdriver he'd left on the television set. He said nothing and neither did I as he pulled both plugs off their flex and put them in his pocket. "The fuse will have blown," he remarked then, and went out of the room.

He returned in a few minutes. "I fixed the fuse." He was carrying two new plugs which he proceeded to attach to the flexes. I watched in silence. He spoke only once and that was to say "You *could* have been killed." I wondered again whether he was speaking with some regret. When he had finished the wiring he connected the two plugs, pushed the extension one in at the wall and turned on the television. "It's all right now," he said.

"What happened, Wesley?" I could still smell burning rubber.

He shook his head, repeated, "It's all right now," then left the room. I watched the wildlife film, then turned the set off but left the plugs connected. He'd said it was all right. He'd handled the connection himself. But I'd take no risks. It was the second mishap I'd had when Wesley was around.

10

OF course, I told Julian. Julian was calling frequently now and I knew it was to see me. So did the others. Mr. Bronson didn't like it, I could tell. But the girls did. They teased me openly but they were pleased at his interest in me and I think Fiona was, too. One day I walked over to the fish and chip shop. Julian made me very welcome, introduced me to his partner Jock and gave me a couple of patties "on the house". The whole atmosphere was friendly, cheerful, and . . . just a little smelly of fish and oil. I hoped he would find some other way to earn his living, then realised I had no right to assume I was going to be involved in his life.

But at least I could confide in him. During his next visit to us, I told him about the plug on the television cord. "I'm afraid Wesley might electrocute himself," not adding "or me", though I suppose that's what I really meant.

"Wesley knows more about electricity than I do," said Julian, puzzled, "and he's perfectly capable of wiring up a plug correctly. Max keeps a stock of electrical fittings and Wesley does all the repairs round the place."

"He could have made a mistake this time."

"It's unlikely. The very fact that his hands are clumsy makes him slow, and for that reason more careful. He's less likely to make an accidental error than a normal person doing the job in a hurry. And wiring up a plug is a very simple operation. Which one was it that burned out? The one on the extension, or the new one he'd just put on the television lead?"

"I don't know. I was a bit startled, and didn't notice at the time. Then Wesley removed both plugs and took them away before he put new ones on."

"Even if it was the extension cord one, it would probably have been Wesley who attached it in the first place. I'll go and have a word with him."

He came back shortly with a grim face. "I can't understand it. Wesley swears he wired up the new plug correctly and the other had been in use for months. So either he'd got the wires mixed in the new one or the extension one had become defective through constant handling. Did you notice any bare wires showing, Pam? Was the outer covering of the flex torn or missing near either plug?"

"I don't think so. When I connected the two I saw no signs of wear in the flex."

"Then Wesley's lying. I asked for the plugs he'd taken off and he said he'd thrown them out. The rubbish bag was taken yesterday. But he wasn't speaking frankly, as he usually does. I felt he was hiding something. Pam, have you offended him? Does he resent your presence here?"

"I'm not sure. He could. Do you think he rigged up that explosion on purpose? Trying to kill me?"

"It wouldn't have killed you unless you had contact with the bare wires. Even if the outer casing is torn, the wires are encased in insulating material. And it wasn't exactly an 'explosion', was it? If it was arranged deliberately he was not trying to burn the house down or annihilate you. But he might have been trying to frighten you away."

"He's very fond of Charis and Diella. Perhaps he doesn't like my being with them so much?"

"I don't understand it at all," said Julian. "It's not like the Wesley I know. He's never been malicious. But there may be depths of feeling which I haven't been aware of. He certainly wouldn't attempt to kill anyone. He knows I don't believe his story and I've warned him. I've threatened him. If anything like that ever happens again . . . I think I got the message through. But please, Pam, be careful."

Then we talked of other things. I'd have liked to tell him about meeting Mr. Smith and what he'd said to me but he looked worried enough already. Besides, I'd explained matters satisfactorily to the man Smith and we'd parted on assumed friendly terms, so there was no real basis for the little fear which kept nagging at me in that regard. I did mention the heroin, though. "Mr. Bronson still mistrusts me. I'm sure he thinks I was smuggling it in."

"Of course he doesn't. Max is a good father and his first concern is naturally for his daughters. He admitted to himself the possibility—that's all, just the mere possibility—that you knew it was in your bag. He thought you may have been asked to bring the package and done so innocently, and then been afraid to admit it to him or the police."

"How do you know? Have you spoken to him about it?"

"Yes. He says you're a pleasant, efficient young lady."

"Then why does he want me to go home early? He suggested I leave as soon as the school holidays are over."

"Well, you won't see much of the girls

then, will you? They'll have sport after school and homework in the evenings. There's not much point in your staying. I dare say you can if you want to. *I* don't want you to go, you know that."

"I think he wants the girls relieved of my company as soon as possible."

I expected Julian to say "Nonsense" or "Of course he doesn't ", but he was silent for a while and then said, disappointingly, "It could be so. Try to see his point of view, Pam. I'm sure he doesn't suspect you of anything but innocent participation in carrying an illicit article. But that to him means that you have a relative or friend or at least an acquaintance who *is* involved in the drug world. And that's enough to a conscientious, caring father to render you a persona non grata. Can't you see that?"

"I suppose so. Everyone knows the heroin was destroyed, don't they?"

"Of course they do. Most people who were told have already forgotten the whole thing. You try and do the same."

"Yes, I shall."

Christmas came, and I was still trying, without any marked success. There were fifteen at the table for the midday Christmas dinner and the atmosphere was jolly. Fiona, her mother-in-law and the girls had prepared the food themselves. I helped a little when I could but I was not asked to. The Merseys, Miss Elliott and Julian came an hour or so before the other guests and we opened our gifts from under the brightly decorated Christmas tree, everyone—not only the girls— shrieking with laughter at some of the ingenious ways which had been devised to spend two dollars.

The meal was sumptuous, a real English dinner, and the weather cool enough for us to enjoy it thoroughly. We had crackers to pull and paper hats to wear, a sparkling New Zealand wine which was equal to the best champagne I'd tasted, chocolates, coffee and liqueurs to end the feast. Everyone was in good humour, Mr. Bronson even addressing me jovially and choosing to pull his cracker with me. Uncle Harry had spent the morning at his favourite pastime, by the look of him, and was red-faced, beaming and affectionate, oozing good cheer and fellowship. After the meal he grabbed me and planted a "Christmas kiss" on me. I wriggled out of his clutch, but then he turned to Wesley, who was alone, and took him off to a corner to talk. I saw Wesley's wide smile and head-nodding, so I guessed it was a topic to his taste, and decided that there were worse things than a tendency to drink too much. If it had been Harry Mersey who had pushed Wesley into the pool last year, he'd done it when he was too far gone to know what he was doing. He was going out of his way now to be kind to Wesley. I knew he would have preferred to be drinking port with some of the guests there. The prevalent goodwill was infectious and I felt well disposed towards Harry Mersey that day.

Julian's shop was closed for three days, so we had his company for each of those days. We swam, we ate, played games and went for picnics. It should have been three days of complete happiness for me. The look in Julian's eye was enough to turn my head, and although the others were present, we talked to each other, argued, compared opinions, discussed food, plants, literature, pastimes, music and life itself. It was amazing how similar our tastes were.

New Year was full of gaiety, too. Visitors, another big meal, a party at night, seeing the New Year in, watching a fireworks display, singing Auld Lang Syne. Julian was there, of course. It was festive, merry, light-hearted. And all the time my uneasiness never left me. Something ominous and sinister was nagging at my mind.

On the third day of the new year, another "incident" occurred. There were two ceiling lights in my bedroom, one in the centre of the room and one hanging over the head of the bed. The latter had no bulb in it. It was not used because a more efficient table lamp had been installed on the desk beside the bed. In the middle of the night, the early hours of the fourth of January, the ceiling lamp fitting and metal shade over my bed fell down. It knocked the outside edge of my pillow before it landed on the floor. I got up, turned on the centre light and examined it. Half the plastic casing of the flex had been pulled away and both wires were cut through. The shade and fitting had been held up by the half of the plastic which had been allowed to remain.

That's when I became not just uneasy, but scared. Because Wesley had been in my room that afternoon, fixing a loose hinge on the wardrobe door. How long would the portion of plastic casing have held? Would one used to dealing with electrical equipment be able to judge to a nicety what time would elapse before it gave way? Wesley did all the electrical repairs in the house. He was more used to handling flex than anyone else there.

The next morning I told the Bronsons what had happened. Wesley was there at the time, having his breakfast, and I looked searchingly at his face for signs of guilt. The one glance he gave me was neither sympathetic nor surprised. Then he reached out for another piece of toast and buttered it slowly. Mr. Bronson and Fiona came into my room with me to examine the cut wires. I asked bluntly, "Is someone here trying to kill me?"

Mr. Bronson shook his head. "This shade would have given you a sore head if it had landed on you, but it wouldn't have killed you."

"Would Wesley know that?"

"Has he been in your room?"

Fiona answered. "Yes, he fixed a hinge for Pamela yesterday. I asked him to. But Wesley wouldn't . . . shall I get an electrician, Max?"

"No, I'll mend it myself when I come home tonight. I am very sorry this happened, Miss Martin. It looks as though Wesley has it in for you, but these stupid attempts to hurt you must stop at once. Don't worry. I'll speak to him and I shan't mince words. There'll be no more of it." He looked very angry.

"What have I done to annoy him?"

"He may simply consider you have too

much influence on Charis and Diella. They like you very much, you know. We were lucky in the choice our London agent made."

Well, *that* was something, coming from him!

No one told the girls that the wires had been tampered with. They assumed it was one of those normal trivial accidents which occur when fittings grow old. But, Mrs. Bronson senior must have known because when we were alone together that morning, she said. "And *now* will you have some sense and go back to England?"

I reminded her, "I'm here for three months."

"Don't be a fool, girl. Go home while you still can."

"What do you mean, Mrs. Bronson?"

"Think about it. You might not be so lucky the fourth time." Then she walked out of the room before I could ask any further questions. Was she threatening me? Did they all want to get rid of me? It might not have been Wesley who was trying to frighten me, but one of the others. Mr. Bronson could have fired me at any time, or merely asked me to leave. *He* wouldn't have to drop a lampshade on my head as persuasion. Fiona—absent, dreamy, one could never be sure about Fiona. But I'd had nothing but kindness from her. Mrs. Bronson was openly urging me to go. Could she have fixed that plug, or the light cord, or cut the rope on the swing? Easily, I decided. She had the opportunity, she was wiry and active still. Then I remembered that I'd been out all day and the door of my flat was left unlocked during the day. Vera? Aunt Mary? Or Harry, the rubicund drunk? It would take only a few seconds to tamper with that light-flex. A little longer to cross the wires on the lounge plug, but they'd all called that day, or was it the day before? I couldn't remember. As for the swing, anyone could have done that, but only Wesley knew he would be swinging me in it. But then, *I* swung *him* at times. No, I always went first, he would count on that. The whole family knew that I often sat on that swing, reading, when I had a few moments to myself. It was not necessarily Wesley who cut the ropes. The girls? Oh no, not the girls. *Please*, not the girls!

Two days after that happened, I saw Mr. Smith the other side of the street, watching the house. It was then I decided to go back to the vicar. After all, he'd invited me to, and he wouldn't worry about me the way Julian would if I told him.

The girls were spending more time with me now. There were fewer than thirty days left of their school holidays, "and then we won't see much of you," said Diella, "so we've got to make the most of it while we can. We'll miss you, Pammy. Do you *have* to go back?"

"Are we speaking any better?" asked Charis.

They were not, as far as I could see. I'd had no influence on their speech at all. But then, there was very little wrong with it to begin with. I was flattered that they wanted me to be with them more often now, but their company made it difficult for me to go and consult Mr. Jarrett. I could hardly pretend that I wanted spiritual guidance and I didn't think it wise to tell them about the causes of the accidents I'd had. It was evident that their father had not told them, so I said nothing myself. I didn't want them to have any suspicions of their Uncle Wesley. He wouldn't harm *them*, I was sure. He was devoted to them. And he might be entirely innocent of all three attempts to injure me.

I had to find some way to see the vicar without causing comment. As we still went to church every Sunday morning I waited until the next occasion and then, as we filed past the vicar on the way out, I said quickly, "May I see you some time, please?"

He nodded and said quietly, "I'll phone." Then he turned to shake hands with the man behind me. It didn't seem very satisfactory, but just after lunch on the same day, the phone rang.

Charis answered it. "It's the vicar for you, Pam."

"What's Pammy done?" asked Diella. "Were you wicked in church, Pammy? Did you yawn during the sermon or show photographs to your neighbour? Or does he want you to join the choir or take a Guides group or . . . ?"

Fiona broke in. "If he does want you to do something like that, Pamela, and you feel like it, please feel free to accept. I'm sure we can fit in with any arrangements."

"Thank you, Fiona." I went to the phone, carefully shutting the door behind me. But I needn't have worried.

"Miss Martin? Are you free this afternoon to come round to the vicarage? Say at about two-thirty? If it's not convenient for you we can arrange some other time."

"I think so, Mr. Jarrett, but I'll check with the family to see if they need me."

I went back to the dining-room and reported what he'd said. "He didn't say what he wanted me for. Is it all right if I go?"

180

"Of course it is," said Fiona. "And you must take my car. It's too far to walk on a hot day like this."

How nice they all were! I was already ashamed of my earlier suspicions when I drove to the vicarage a little later.

11

" A DRUG syndicate," said the vicar, "is a highly organised hierarchy, with the management at the top, the suppliers, the couriers, the distributors, and at the bottom of the pyramid, the peddlers. If your Mr. Smith were a supplier he would not be interested in the small packet you had brought in. If he were a peddler he would not be concerned with supplies. Those who make the final deliveries are under strict orders which they dare not disobey. They do their rounds as directed—pubs, park benches, massage parlours and other pre-arranged points. As long as this man is working alone, I don't think you need worry too much. Why not report the matter to the police?"

"They think I'm a criminal. They wouldn't listen to me if I said I suspected someone else. Besides, this man hasn't *done* anything. I could only say he called to see me and he phoned and he looked at the house one day."

"You underestimate the intelligence of our police force. I had a word with the detective-inspector I know and he made some enquiries. The fact that you were in possession of heroin has certainly been recorded, but so has your claim that it was without your knowledge. However, I see why you are reluctant to be questioned again. You say this man has a legitimate business in Otahuhu. Most drug principals hide behind a legitimate business, but the behaviour of this man is not that of one in control of a drug ring. If he is trying to cash in on the game by himself, he would naturally be alarmed if he thought you were going to walk into his office and give him away to his business colleagues. You tell me you satisfactorily explained your presence in the building."

"Oh yes, you see I . . ." I was going to tell him about seeing Mr. Smith pick up the wrong case on the bus, but the vicar spoke again.

"He may live in your district, and could have been passing, pausing to look at the house, wondering whether to approach you. However, if he contacts you again, let me know. I think it would then be a matter for the police. But you didn't come to see me because you saw a man looking at the house you're living in. There's more than that worrying you."

I don't know how he knew, but I admitted, "Yes, it's the Bronsons. They brought me all the way out here and now I think they want to get rid of me. Julian says Mr. Bronson wouldn't want the slightest risk that his daughters should associate with someone even innocently connected with drugs."

"Julian is right. That would be the normal reaction of a devoted father."

"But Mr. Bronson can just tell me to go. Any time. That's simple. They're trying to *scare* me away. Well, one of them is." I told him about the three accidents. He questioned me closely.

"And in each case, you could have been hurt but not killed. You suspect Wesley, then?"

"He's the one most likely to have done it in every case but I can't be sure. It could be any of them. Old Mrs. Bronson wants me to go home. She tells me so to my face. Miss Elliott or the Merseys *could* have done it. They had an opportunity each time. I hate to think it's the girls, but it's possible. The whole family could be ganging up on me, trying to frighten me away. Or did they bring me out to have the fun of killing me off? The next accident might not be so harmless and Mrs. Bronson actually told me so, as if she was threatening me. I know I must sound silly and hysterical to you, but I'm so puzzled about it all."

He didn't laugh at me. He said thoughtfully, "I don't know the family very well, except for Mrs. Bronson senior, who is an intelligent, perceptive woman, and Julian, whom I note you do not include in your list of suspects. The girls join in a few of the social activities which we organise but they don't come to Bible Class or Youth groups so I have had little opportunity to talk with them. The parents occasionally attend a service. Maxwell Bronson is a successful businessman and I know nothing against him. His brother is mentally retarded and one can never be sure what goes on within a damaged mind. Or within any mind, in fact," he added. "But I have not heard of any incidents of violence on his part. In all, they appear to be a respected, decent-living family."

"Why did they pay all that money to bring me out here?"

"That is not necessarily a cause for suspicion," he said. "For one thing, the amount of your return fare and your salary seems a lot of money to you but means little to the Bronsons. Mr. Bronson controls several thriving businesses and his brother Wesley is extremely wealthy."

"Even so, I can't see the sense in it. Bringing me out to teach their daughters to speak as if they'd been to Oxford. It's just snobbery."

"Don't be too hard on them. Why blame anyone who wishes to cultivate the mark of a famous University which he never had the opportunity to attend himself? It is commendable to emulate what is good, is it not? To strive for perfection? The sound of a well-educated English voice is pleasing to the ear. Mr. Bronson may wish his girls to assume it not as a false claim to superiority but simply because it is harmonious."

"But there are elocution schools here."

"Yes, but it may be that your influence was to be unforced, incidental, and therefore acceptable by two teenage girls who are at a stage of life when dictates of parents are often defied."

"They don't speak badly."

"They are none the less exposed to the New Zealand accent, which is ugly, and which, unfortunately, television actors sometimes assume deliberately as if it were a matter of pride, exaggerating and flaunting its deficiencies. You are in a country where clear speech is not an aim in life. Even some of our news announcers make two syllables of the word *known*, and refer to 'next Feberry' or 'the seckertry' of a Union. Yes, I can understand a sensitive soul with a heavy purse taking steps to deter his children from adopting the prevalent mode of speech."

He spoke clearly and precisely himself. I argued, "How did they know I could influence the girls? How could they predict that the girls would even like me or consent to be with me? As a matter of fact, I don't think their speech has improved one bit while I've been here."

"One does not buy a commodity with any certainty of its . . ."

I had to interrupt then. "Mr. Jarrett!"

He stopped and looked at me enquiringly.

"Mr. Jarrett, I listen to your sermon every Sunday morning and you mean every word. Now you're . . . you're just *talking*."

He stared at me for a few seconds and then laughed. "You are an astute young woman and you're perfectly right. I *have* been just talking, arguing, putting forth a possibility, trying to convince myself as well as you that bringing you twelve thousand miles was a natural thing to do. I, too, find it strange. But then I am often surprised at other people's priorities, as we all are, simply because they are not our own. I don't like avocado pears or toheroa soup, yet I recognise that they are considered delicacies by many."

"Oh, what can I do? Old Mrs. Bronson has told me quite bluntly to go home."

"So did I, if you remember."

"Yes, but for a different reason. And now Wesley or one of them is trying to hurt me or scare me, if not kill me. It's making me jittery and fanciful and sometimes I wonder if I've been brought out for some horrible purpose. Like being murdered."

Mr. Jarrett looked thoughtful, stroked his chin and murmured, *"Wanted a governess, must be young."*

I knew he had a habit of quoting the Bible but I hadn't known the ancient Hebrews talked about governesses. "Is

189

that from the Old Testament?" I asked him.

He laughed at me. "No, it's the typical opening sentence of certain mystery romances which were popular at the turn of the century. I was not around then but the phrase was still quoted by my parents when I was a schoolboy and there were actually a couple of old volumes in the house which I was not permitted to read and therefore did. They were much of a kind. A young, innocent girl would be lured by an advertisement into a dark mansion of twisting corridors, locked rooms, wailing madwomen, lecherous employers and evil ghosts."

I knew he was trying to cheer me up by making the whole thing seem ridiculous, fictional, and letting me realise how my imagination had run away with me. My common sense was coming back. I said, "The Bronson house isn't a bit like that. It's sunny and cheerful and nice and so are they. I'm sure they are, really. They just don't like *me* any more. All those accidents were . . . just accidents. Wesley wouldn't hurt anyone."

"Now don't go to the other extreme and be over-confident or trusting."

"The dog's devoted to all of them and animals know, don't they?"

The vicar frowned and then said in his pedantic, rather pompous manner, "It is erroneously assumed that animals have an innate ability to judge character in humans. But how can one know what attracts a dog to one man rather than to his neighbour? It may be that one smells more like a dead rat than the other. Or if it is really a personality trait which the dog discerns, it may not be that of integrity or kindness. Dogs are by nature hunters and certain other qualities would presumably win their respect. Sly cunning, for instance, must be an admirable quality by animal standards."

"I see what you mean. But there are people, too. Mr. and Mrs. Bronson have lots of visitors, dinner guests and so on."

"The poor is hated even of his own neighbour but the rich hath many friends.

I don't say that is the explanation but one must bear the fact in mind."

"I still like them. I like them all. Except the clock in the hall. I just *hate* that clock. Its *tock* is louder than its *tick*. Oh dear, I'm getting silly and neurotic again. I assure you, Mr. Jarrett, I was quite a matter-of-fact sensible person when I came here and I was perfectly happy until that box of powder was found." I got to my feet. "Well, thank you very much for listening to me. It really has helped to talk about it. I guess I just . . ."

"Wait. What box of powder?"

"The heroin. You know."

"You didn't say anything about a *box*. Are you telling me that the heroin found in your bag was in a *box?*"

"Yes, a little cardboard box. The lid came off, you see, and it spilled. That's what started it all. I was happy until then."

"Sit down. How large a box? Show me."

I measured with my thumb and forefinger. "About that size, round. Like a pill box. Does it matter?"

"Yes, it does matter. It matters considerably. Why didn't you tell me this before? You spoke of a small paper packet."

"No, that was what Mr. Bronson took to the chemist and the police. A little sample. He burned the box and he wiped out my bag for me."

"Why didn't he take the box to the police?"

"He thought it was insecticide and could be dangerous to handle. Does it really matter how it was packed?"

He was looking very grave. "Have you any idea what price heroin fetches on the market? A box that size, full of it, would be worth thousands of dollars if it were pure. Can you imagine anyone planting that amount in your bag and making no effort to retrieve it?"

"They'd know it was burned. Whoever spread the story wouldn't have left that bit out. I suppose it was someone at the disco where the girls go, or a party at the home of one of their friends."

"*I* didn't know it was burned. I wish you had told me about this when you first consulted me on the matter."

"If it's worth so much, I guess that's why the man came to see me."

"Your Mr. Smith? Yes. I don't think we've taken that episode seriously enough. A pill box, full of heroin. Good heavens! You tell me Mr. Bronson took a small sample and then wiped out your bag. Thoroughly?"

"Yes, he was awfully nice about it until he had the sample he took analysed and found it was pure heroin."

"That would certainly be a shock."

"He thought it was insecticide, like I said. He went to a lot of trouble to get rid of it all so that I couldn't touch any and be poisoned. He said it would be highly concentrated and even a speck could kill. So he burned my tissues and cleaned up everything else in my bag for me."

"What were you carrying in your bag?"

"A cardigan—we washed that—and slippers, but they were in a plastic bag so they were all right. And a book."

"You have the book still?"

"Yes, Mr. Bronson wiped it over carefully, all the edges, too."

"And that was all? No handkerchiefs? Scarfs? Anything that may not have been wiped entirely clear of the powder?"

"I had tissues and Mr. Bronson burned them. Nothing else. My make-up was in my handbag."

"Nothing else at all? Nothing which might have a trace of the powder still adhering to it?"

"No. Oh, except Talbot. I was forgetting Talbot. A photo he gave me just before I went through the last door at the airport. I slipped that into my pocket because I didn't want them to see it, because I don't really like him. I told you."

"Where is that photo now?"

"Still in the pocket of my suit."

"Was it near the top of your bag?

Could it have had any of the powder on it?"

"It was covered in it. I was going to wipe it and then throw it away but when I discovered the powder was only heroin I didn't bother."

"*Only* heroin! I want you to bring me that suit coat with the photo in the pocket. Bring the whole coat. Be careful not to drop the photo out or to touch it."

"But they've tested the powder, Mr. Jarrett. The chemist and the police both tested the sample Mr. Bronson took. It was just heroin, not poison."

"Heroin *is* poison, young woman. Poison of the deadliest kind." He was looking fierce. "Please do as I ask you, and as soon as you can. Today if possible. I'll be home all afternoon. Bring me that coat and tell no one you are doing so."

"Not even Julian?"

"Certainly not Julian."

"All right. I'll get it to you. I don't really see why you want it, but I'll bring it."

"Good. By the way, would you care to take a class in our Sunday school?"

"I'd rather not."

"I didn't imagine you would. But you may tell the Bronsons that I invited you to."

12

THE girls had gone out by the time I'd driven home. Mr. Bronson and Wesley were in the back garden, trimming the lawn edges, and both gave me a friendly wave when I walked round the side of the house. Mrs. Bronson was sitting in a deck chair near the back door and nodded to me. "How's the vicar? Keeping well?"

"He looks it."

"What did he want you for?"

"He asked if I'd like to take a Sunday school class."

"He could have done that over the phone. All right, it's your own business. But if he gave you any advice, you take it, girl. He knows what he's talking about, that man."

I passed through to the kitchen where Fiona was bottling peaches. She said cheerfully, "Hullo, Pam. Julian rang while you were away. He can't come round today. He's helping a friend paint his boat." No question about why the vicar wanted me. Fiona didn't pry.

"I left the car out in case you wanted it later, Fiona."

"A good idea. We might go for a drive before dinner, if you'd like to. The girls won't be home until seven."

Friendly, welcoming conversation, as if I were one of the family. None of them could be deliberately trying to hurt me. "Can I help you, Fiona?"

"No, thanks, Pam. This is a one-man job. Why not get a book and relax out in the sun? This lovely weather's not going to last."

The phone rang then. "I'll get it," I said and went through to the hall.

"Miss Martin? Don't hang up on me, please. I want to apologise."

I didn't slam down the receiver. If what he said was true I should at least have the courtesy to listen. I merely said coldly, "Yes, Mr. Smith?"

"I made a mistake about you and I'm

very sorry I bothered you as I did. I shan't do it again. I wanted to assure you of that and to thank you again for your kindness the other day in coming to let me know I had the wrong case. The one I'd picked up was full of brushes—hair brushes, tooth brushes, all sorts. Some hawker's samples. I took it to the bus depot and was lucky enough to collect my own from there the next day."

"That's good," I said politely.

"By the way, one of the men I was with when you called the other day thought he'd met you once at a birthday party in Richmond. Jim Merton, it was. The tall fair one."

"You weren't with a fair man when I saw you, Mr. Smith. There was just one other man in your office."

"Oh, is that so? We were so busy that morning—so many callers. How disappointing. It must have been later that I saw Jim. Who was there when you came up? Are you sure it wasn't Jim?"

"It was a plump, dark-haired man."

"Oh, who would that be now? What

did he look like? It could have been Brett. A fellow with a beard?"

"No, he didn't have a beard. He had a scar on his cheek. I'm sure I've never met him in Richmond. I remember faces well and I'd never seen him before. And I don't know the name Jim Merton at all."

"Well, it's not important. He just thought he'd like to renew his acquaintance with you and I said I'd ask because I wanted to phone you anyway. As I said, to apologise. I give you my word that I will not approach you again. Thank you once more for your trouble. I hope you'll enjoy the rest of your stay in New Zealand."

"Thank you, Mr. Smith." What else could I say?

"Well, good-bye, Miss Martin." Then he hung up.

I felt very relieved, so much so that I had the cheek to go and ask Fiona if I could use the car again. "It's something the vicar wants." I knew she wouldn't ask what, and she'd assume it had been the vicar on the phone.

"Of course you may, Pam. You know that."

I went to my flat, collected my suit coat from the wardrobe and left by the front door, where the others could not see me carrying it. I felt sure now that my suspicions of them were unfounded but Mr. Jarrett had been emphatic that no one must know I was taking it to him.

He was home and luckily no one else was with him. He took the photo out and looked at it. "So that's Talbot?"

"Yes. Oh, I know he *looks* interesting."

The vicar didn't answer. He was fingering the frame, touching the parts where powder showed. Then he tapped the frame gently and let some of the white powder fall on the table, took up a pinch between his finger and thumb and rubbed it to and fro, then smelt it.

"The man who calls himself Smith rang me up," I told him. "He apologised for bothering me and said he won't contact me again."

The vicar looked up sharply. "Did he? I hope he meant it."

"He sounded as if he did. He said he'd made a mistake about me and he gave me his word that he wouldn't phone or call again. So that's all right."

The vicar was staring at the photo again. "I'll keep this for a while. Don't tell anyone you brought it to me. I'll be in touch with you later. In the meantime, my advice to you is the same as it was. Fly home."

"Oh, I was just silly and upset this morning, Mr. Jarrett. Imagining all sorts of things. I'm over that now."

"I think you should leave the Bronson's house, Pamela. If you won't go back to England, at least find other lodgings. Leave their employment."

I was shocked. "You mean I'm really in danger?"

He was looking very serious. "There's something going on and I don't like it. I have the glimmerings of a theory and I don't like that either."

"They really want to kill me?"

"No, no. Your life is not at risk." But he looked terribly worried as he said it. "You were not brought out here to be killed."

"They're just trying to frighten me?"

"If my theory is correct, no one is trying to frighten you."

"Then I don't understand. . . ?"

"Neither do I, Pamela. I sincerely hope that the only explanation which occurs to me is not the correct one. I wish I could persuade you to take the next flight home."

How I wish now that I had listened to that very wise advice! At the time I protested rapidly. "I can't. I haven't nearly enough money to pay my own fare back and I'm not going to wire my family for it because they didn't want me to come and that would be like admitting that I'd made a mistake. Anyway, I *didn't* make a mistake. The Bronsons are a very nice family and . . ."

He broke in. "In other words, you've fallen for my organist."

"Oh, all right. I guess that's what I

really mean. I can't leave him now, Mr. Jarrett. Not yet. We're just getting to know each other."

"Very well. I see I can't persuade you, but I don't like your remaining in that house. Listen to me. If ever you do feel endangered, if anything unusual occurs which frightens you, if you feel you need help, wish someone else were present, someone to support you, send me a message and I'll come at once."

It sounded a bit melodramatic after he'd just told me I was not in any danger. "Oh, I couldn't do that. Interrupt your work? There's always Julian."

"Who would be frying potato chips. Don't worry about disturbing me. If you feel in danger, phone me or let me know by some means. I'm serious about this."

"You mean if you're in the middle of communion or a sermon and one of your sidesmen hands you up a note saying 'I'm scared' you'd lay down your Bible and say 'Excuse me, folks. Take five. I've got another job on right now.'?"

He didn't smile. He said, "As a matter

of fact, I would. That is how gravely I regard this matter." He meant it. He was dead serious, gazing at me with those steady, expressive eyes.

I pointed out, "If I *was* in trouble and suspected one of the family I could hardly phone you up and say so. They'd hear me."

"Then we'd better have a simple code. What would you suggest?"

"I don't know. Anything. Some way of telling you I need help. I know! What was that hymn we had last Sunday about skidding in the mud?"

He smiled a little then, just a small upward turn of his lips. "I suppose you are referring to number 300 in the Ancient and Modern?" He quoted

"Be thou my guardian and my
    guide
And hear me when I call.
Let not my slippery footsteps
    slide
And hold me lest I fall.

It was not the local vicar who was being appealed to for help. But no matter, if that is what you fancy. Refer to that hymn, or its number, 300, and I'll understand."

"I wouldn't do it unless I was really scared."

"I know that. But don't be afraid of giving a false alarm. If that message ever comes to me, be assured I'll make all haste."

Which was jolly decent of him, I thought as I drove home. It wouldn't ever be necessary now, of course. I wasn't afraid any more. I'd just been neurotic and silly, upset by a few little accidents which couldn't have done me any harm anyway . . .

13

"**W**HEN are you going home, girl?"

I answered bluntly, "Why do you want me to, Mrs. Bronson?"

"I think it advisable that you go soon," said the old lady. "We discussed this before. It may not be good for you to stay here the full three months."

"Why, Mrs. Bronson? Please say what you mean more clearly."

"You may be . . . hurt, if you stay here," she said more gently. "I'd like you to go soon."

I supposed she was thinking of the accidents I'd had. "I don't think I run any risk of being badly hurt," I said. "I'll be on my guard now."

"Huh."

"Is Wesley conscious of being different from other men?" I asked her. "Does it worry him? Make him bitter?"

"I don't think he minds being different from the majority of men but he is deeply aware that he is mentally inferior to his brother and he knows it was not always so."

"I suppose one is always more envious of a close relative than of a stranger."

"Yes, one can feel indifference towards an outsider, but feelings are more intense within a family. The close tie between brothers can turn to fierce hatred if one is less favoured than the other. Envy festers and grows. The old story of the have-nots and the haves. Cain killed his brother because the spiteful petty-minded god of that particular tale spurned his gift of first-fruits in favour of Abel's fat lamb. Esau swore vengeance on Jacob because Jacob worked a swindle to get his father's blessing. Joseph was envied and disliked by all his brothers because he had a many-coloured coat and they didn't. History is full of such instances. Envy turning to hatred. Then others, innocent outsiders, can get hurt."

Fiona came in. "Mr. Jarrett's just rung,

Pam. He'd like you to pop round to the vicarage this afternoon. He's free between two and three and wants to see you. I said you'd come. You can have the car. I'm not going out until late."

"But the girls and I were going . . ."

"The girls can wait. You mustn't think you're at their beck and call, Pam. It's not as though you even have a day off from your work."

"It's not work at all," I assured her. "It's like one long holiday. But I'll go if you think it best."

"Give the vicar my regards," said Mrs. Bronson.

I accepted Fiona's offer of the car and drove to the vicarage after lunch, remembering it was Monday and supposed to be the vicar's day off. Decent of the old boy to spend time on my problems.

"Mrs. Bronson senior sends her regards," I told him.

"How is she? I have not been to see her for a while."

"She's very well and active."

"I'm glad to hear it. She doesn't come

to church now but she used to do so regularly. A remarkable woman. She took a Bible Study group for us."

"*She* did?" I was surprised. "She told me this morning that the god of Cain and Abel was spiteful and petty."

Unexpectedly he nodded. "Indeed yes. I would add feeble-minded and vicious. Mrs. Bronson was one of the few to whom I could safely entrust Old Testament studies. So many simple souls accept that part of the Bible as the dictates of their Creator instead of what it is—the history of the early tribes of Israel and their spiritual development. Their ideas of the great Jehovah varied but in the main the fellow was bloodthirsty, cruel and vengeful, a tyrant who didn't know the meaning of the word *love*. And the characters who are so often referred to with reverence were indeed fashioned in his image. Samuel, for instance, who chopped poor Agag into pieces, David— you know the story of Bathsheba, the prophets—like Elisha, who was getting a bit thin on top and when called 'Baldie' by a group of small children, summoned a she-bear from the woods to tear them all up. I really think the Old Testament should be banned for all readers except students of history or theology. The tales are full of revenge and murder, often ordered by the god in vogue at the time. Of course, there is much that is wise and good within its pages. Properly interpreted, it is of immense value, as human nature has remained the same from that day to this."

"That's what Mrs. Bronson implied. She was talking of the brothers in it—the hate felt by one who was deprived of what another had. Cain and Abel, Jacob and Esau."

"*A brother offended is harder to be won than a strong city*. I could add other examples to those Mrs. Bronson quoted. But you are not here for Bible study."

"It must be just awful for Mrs. Bronson seeing a son like that."

"Yes. *A foolish son is a grief to his father and a bitterness to her that bare him*. Much of the unhappiness in the world is caused by children who develop in a way their parents deplore. But I must not keep you talking about such generalities. You will want to get back to your young charges. I'm sorry I had to ask you to come, but I am expecting callers myself and I hesitated to phone in case you were not alone. What I have to say is not for others' ears."

He paused and I waited. Then he went on, "There was enough powder on that photograph for me to have it analysed."

"Oh yes?" I said politely. Mr. Bronson had already had it analysed so I didn't know why Mr. Jarrett had bothered. I didn't like to ask him. You don't accuse the vicar of being a silly old fusspot.

"I have had the results phoned through to me but both your suit jacket and the photograph are still with my chemist friend. I'll return them to you later."

"There's no hurry."

"Now listen to me carefully. You are not to go out alone with Wesley again. You are never to be alone with him in the house or anywhere else. Make sure there is always a third person present."

"Why, Mr. Jarrett? You don't really think. . . ? He's not going to. . . ?"

"Please do as I say. It's very important."

He was waiting for me to agree. I was very disappointed, because I still liked Wesley, with his big brown eyes and his slow, shy smile, and I had found it hard to believe what Mr. Bronson and his mother had said. Now even the vicar was warning me.

"Do you hear what I say, Pamela?" He spoke sharply, as if to one of his choir boys. "You're to do as I say. At all times avoid being alone with Wesley."

"All right," I said meekly. "I don't understand, but I'll do as you say."

"Good. Now, one other thing, more pleasant to discuss. The young people of St. Bernard's put on a play in March each year, usually a comedy. Something light, which will appeal to children's and old folks' institutions. You will not be here then to take a part, but if you care to come to rehearsals to help with stage arrangements or costumes or other matters, we would be very happy to have you. Charis and Diella usually take an active part, if not in the actual play, in the preparations and organisation. We try to involve as many as possible."

"Thank you, Mr. Jarrett." I realised he was again giving me a reason for asking me to call, but I might very well accept the invitation and go to a few rehearsals.

I had driven only a couple of blocks towards the Bronsons when I stopped the car, deciding to turn round and go back. I'd meant to ask his advice about Mr. Smith, because I'd been doing some thinking in the night and I didn't like the conclusions I'd come to. What the vicar had said about Wesley had put it out of my head, but I really wanted his advice again. Because that man Smith had lied to me. He had not been with anyone when he came out of his office, and there was only one man there when I looked in. That was the plump dark one with the scar. So how *could* his friend Jim Merton have seen me? From another room? But a businessman wouldn't be so scatty as to forget the callers he'd had and which one was with him at that particular time. He could have made up that story as an excuse for phoning me, something to start with so that I wouldn't hang up in his ear when he really wanted to apologise. But I doubted it. Another thing—would a travelling salesman keep his brushes in an attaché case? The Buntings man who used to come to our door carried a suitcase. He'd flip the lid open and display an array of sample brushes all fastened neatly into place. How would one get on with a despatch bag? Tip them all out in a heap on the doorstep? Even in New Zealand, they wouldn't be so badly organised. That whole phone conversation, now I had thought it over, smelt fishy. And I couldn't forget the look on his face when he'd said "Do you know what happens to snoopers?" If I could discuss it all with the vicar again, he'd tell me what to do and whether it was anything to worry about and if I should really go to the police.

Then I remembered it was his day off and I'd already taken up half an hour of his time. He was expecting callers, too. I'd have to postpone my consultation until some other time. I drove home.

14

"**W**HAT did he want, Pammy?"
"Did you audition for the choir?"

"He asked me if I'd like to help behind the scenes in the play you're putting on in March. Just until I go."

"Oh yes, that's good fun," said Diella. "We'll be starting on it soon. It's not a Bible story or anything like that. It's usually a lively comedy and we go round old people's Homes and hospital wards hoping it'll cheer them up. Mr. Jarrett always chooses one with a large cast so that as many as possible can join in."

I was grateful to the vicar for giving me this explanation of my visit to him. I didn't want the girls to think there were any secrets between us. I was becoming really fond of those two and I felt sure they liked me, too. The difference in our ages was no handicap to affection. In fact it intensified the bond that was growing. We were near enough in age to enjoy many activities together, yet I was sufficiently older for them to consult me and confide in me.

There were only two weeks of their holidays left now and they kept thinking of places they wanted to show me. "We can see our friends any time," said Charis, "but we shan't have you much longer. Oh, I wish you could stay on."

"*Would* you stay, Pammy?" asked Diella. "I'm going to ask Dad if you can. Just another few months?"

I would have been pleased to. I couldn't bear the thought of leaving Julian. But I knew too well what their father would say to the suggestion.

The next week was very full. We went out every day and Wesley usually came with us. He behaved very well, as always. I knew, even from my own limited reading, that those with any mental impairment are unpredictable in be-haviour. But then, aren't we all? It's not that I disregarded the warnings of the vicar and Mr. Bronson and his mother. The vicar had worked in a mental hospital and should know what he was talking about. But he *could* be wrong. He'd admitted that he didn't know the family very well.

I asked Fiona her opinion one day when the subject came up. She'd said, "I'm glad Wesley is going out with you these days, Pam. He's grown just as attached to you as the rest of us and realises you have so little time left." No invitation to stay longer, but that, I guessed, was because of her husband's veto.

"Yes, and he seems to enjoy the outings," I said. "Mr. Bronson told me he has fits of temper but I've seen no evidence of them. Is it very bad when it occurs?"

"He went for Max one day. I wasn't there myself but Max says it came as a surprise to him and he's been wary ever since. He's well built and more than a match for Wesley normally but he was taken unawares, he told me. I suppose that's why he thought he'd better prepare you for a possible attack of temper. There's always been a bit of resentment present, of course."

"Wesley knows he's not normal," I agreed, "but he seems to accept it. The resentment must just break out under real pressure."

She looked at me strangely, seemed about to speak, then changed her mind. She would never say ill of anyone. Dreamy, but always kind in her words. I would miss her as much as I'd miss the girls.

Julian called in when he could find time and the girls, bless them, left me with him on each occasion. They suspected a romance and Diella hinted that it would suit them very well if I married their uncle and stayed in New Zealand. I hadn't discussed the Smith man with Julian again, or confessed my underlying fear concerning him. The vicar was the expert. I'd have another talk with him soon, so it was unnecessary to worry Julian as well.

One morning he called briefly. Fiona had taken her mother-in-law out for the day. Wesley, the girls and I were sitting in the sun at the back door.

"I'm on my way to the vicarage," said Julian. "I have to see Mr. Jarrett about the music for a wedding coming up shortly so I thought I'd just say hullo in passing."

"Coming directly south-east when the vicarage is north-west," remarked Charis. "Of course. Naturally. You just happened to be passing the gate . . ."

"That's enough from you," said Julian.

"As a matter of fact, you could give us a lift," said Charis. "We have to see him, too, about the play in March. Will he be home now?"

"He'd better be. He told me to come this morning. Yes, of course I'll take you. What about you, Pam? Come, too?"

"I'll stay," I offered. There would be no chance of talking to the vicar while they were all there. "Don't you remember, girls, your father wanted you to pay Mr. Hitchens when he comes?"

"Oh bother, yes. But he might not come until this afternoon. I'll phone Dad."

Charis went inside and returned in a few minutes. "Dad says he's not sure when Mr. Hitchens is coming but he'd like him to get his money and he'd be very glad if you'd stay and pay him. I suggested we leave the money with Uncle Wes but he says he doesn't know the exact amount owing and there may be change to give. He doesn't like to put responsibility like that onto Uncle Wesley. You know where the money jar is, don't you, Pam? And Dad said tell you that if Uncle Harry calls, he can just help himself to the tools he wants to borrow. There's no need for you to go outside and see him."

Thoughtful of him. So he'd noticed my distaste for Harry Mersey? Even if Mr. Bronson didn't trust me, he always showed consideration for my feelings.

I realised when they'd left that I was doing just what the vicar had urged me not to. I was alone with Wesley. Not that

I was frightened over that. I simply couldn't believe that he'd harm me and if he attempted to, I was now on my guard and was confident that I could either restrain him or run. No, I was annoyed because the girls would tell Mr. Jarrett that they'd left me with Wesley and he'd think I had just ignored what he'd said. That wasn't true. When you take up the time of a man as busy as he is to ask advice, the least you can do is respect it, even if you don't agree with it. I'd refused to go home to England as he suggested, but that was different. I think he understood that. But I really had intended to avoid being alone with Wesley, simply to please the old chap. It seemed so discourteous and arrogant to disregard what he'd stressed so firmly. I felt most uncomfortable about it.

Well, Wesley was out on the bench by the pool gazing at the floating leaves, as he so often did. Chief was not with him. Chief had gone for a stroll to meet his neighbourhood friends, as *he* so often did. I decided to do a little weeding on the border round the side of the house; not the side where the path was, leading round to the back, but the other, not used so often and therefore a little more neglected. The soil was fertile and the weeds grew quickly.

It was pleasant in the sun. I looked round the corner of the house once and Wesley was still sitting quietly by the pool. I must have been working there for half an hour or more when I was startled by a loud shout, "Pamela! Come here!" It was the vicar's voice and it sounded urgent. It came from the back garden. I jumped up and ran round, to see Wesley in the swimming pool and the vicar leaning over the side, holding him up. When he saw me he called, "Quick! See to Wesley. Get him out." Then he placed Wesley's hand on the side edge of the bath and ran into the trees at the back of the section. I had a glimpse of another figure, who seemed to be trying to climb the dividing fence. I heard a scuffle and voices, as I raced towards the pool. Wesley's hand was slipping off the edge.

"It's all right, Wesley." I took hold of his hand and pulled him slowly down to the steps at the shallow end, where he climbed out, looking more puzzled than frightened.

Then the vicar was coming towards us from the bushes. He was limping and dishevelled. "Go and change into dry clothes, Wesley," he said, and his calm, matter-of-fact air suggested that falling into a swimming pool was a trivial thing that could happen to anyone in the course of a normal day. It certainly served to comfort Wesley, who merely remarked, "I got pushed in," in a tone of surprise. "Like last year."

"Yes, but it'll never happen again," said Mr. Jarrett. "You're not hurt. Your coat buoyed you up and you were very sensible when I told you to take hold of the edge. You knew just what you had to do."

"Yes, I did, didn't I?" beamed Wesley. "It wasn't bad in the water after all."

The vicar must have known, as I knew, that Wesley's hand would have slipped off the edge in another few seconds, as his clothes weighted with water. If the vicar had not been there, Wesley would surely have drowned. I would not have noticed a mere splash or gasp from where I was at the side of the house, and you cannot give a loud shout when your mouth is full of water. Should I have been keeping an eye on him? He wasn't my responsibility and I'd been assured that he was quite safe on his favourite bench.

But I didn t have time to blame myself. The vicar was busy doing it for me. When Wesley went in to change, he turned to me angrily. "I *told* you not to be alone with Wesley. I made it perfectly clear . . ."

"You're hurt," I said weakly.

"Why didn't you do as you were told?"

"What happened? I don't understand. Who else was there? Wesley says he was pushed."

"Of course he was. If Charis hadn't told me that you'd been left alone with him and that others had been informed of the fact . . . get in my car and drive me home."

He was exceedingly angry and his voice so authoritative that I didn't argue. I did say, "Will Wesley be all right?"

"Yes. He's not even unduly frightened. He can be left. But if I had not walked round the house at that precise moment. . . ! At least you acted promptly when I called and brought him out of the pool efficiently. I had my own hands full." Then he asked more politely, "I'll have to ask you to take me home. I've ricked my ankle and I doubt if I can drive."

"Yes." I nearly said, "Yes, sir," I felt so subdued. He refused to let me help him to the front. He hung onto shrubs, then the fence and hopped into his car. Then he handed me the keys. The gears were similar in arrangement to those of Fiona's Mirage. I knew the way to the vicarage and although I was nervous of making a mistake, as I felt his anger beside me, I drove into the vicarage driveway without incident. He hadn't spoken the whole way.

He climbed out of the car and hobbled into the house. "Come in," he growled. I followed and watched as he sank into a chair and stretched out one leg.

"It's not broken, is it?" I enquired.

"No, but it's sprained and that's going to be a blasted nuisance." I didn't think that was at all a nice way for a vicar to speak.

"What will you do then? Shall I phone for a doctor? They say hot and cold water in turns . . . have you an elastic bandage? Shall I take your shoe off?"

"Stop fussing, woman. If you want to be useful, make a pot of tea. But first go into my study and phone Julian. He should be home by now. He and the girls left when I did. I had to cut short their visit when I heard you were with Wesley."

"But *I* didn't hurt him."

"Thank heaven I didn't wait here one moment longer. We just averted a tragedy. Tell Julian I'd like him to come here as soon as possible."

I couldn't see how it was in any way my fault that Wesley had had a near escape from drowning. But I didn't protest. I did as he asked. Julian was back at the shop and told me he had dropped the girls at the Newmarket shopping centre where they wanted to look at some skirts that had been advertised. They had met some friends there and would not be home until late afternoon. He didn't ask why he was wanted but said he'd come at once.

He must have driven like the devil. I suppose he knew the vicar wouldn't send for him in working hours unless it was something important. I'd only just made the tea and found cups and a tray and taken it all into the lounge when I heard his car pull up. I let him in.

"What's up?" said Julian. "Oh, are you hurt, vicar?"

"Only a sprained ankle," said Mr. Jarrett. He'd taken off his shoe and put his foot up on a stool and didn't look quite so fierce now.

"For which he blames me," I said bitterly.

He turned on me. "I blame you only for not doing as you were asked to do. *A fair woman without discretion is like unto* . . . well, perhaps that simile is a little harsh. I certainly do not blame you for the results of my own clumsiness in tripping over a root while grappling with another person."

"He'd come to borrow tools," I told him. "I suppose he just saw Wesley sitting there and pushed him in, the same as last year at the barbecue. Perhaps he didn't know that Wesley can't swim."

The vicar did not comment on that. He finished his tea rather hurriedly and then said, "I have to go out now. I want you both to stay here until I come back."

"You can't drive with that ankle," I protested. "Shall I come?"

"You'll stay here."

"Shall I phone for a taxi?"

"No, I'll manage. The initial pain is wearing off."

"Can't I take you where you want to go?" asked Julian.

"No, thank you. I prefer to go alone. Stay here and keep an eye on this imbecilic female." His words were not too polite but his eyes were kinder now. "She is utterly unreliable and needs to be permanently looked after."

"I'll bear that in mind," said Julian, and took hold of my hand.

"I'm supposed to be at the Bronsons'," I said, "waiting for Mr. Hitchens, the gardener, to come for his money."

"He can call again," said the vicar. "You are both to remain here."

"Is it really important that you go out now? Your ankle . . ."

"Yes, it is important," he said. "I am going in order to talk, by arrangement, with the person who pushed Wesley into the swimming pool. Perhaps you would fetch me a left-foot slipper from my wardrobe, Julian?"

15

WHEN the vicar had left I explained to Julian what had happened. "It was Harry Mersey. The vicar just caught him doing it but he couldn't chase him right away because he had to save Wesley. He called out to me and then left Wesley to me while he got Harry, just as he was climbing the fence, I think. There was an awful scuffle and the vicar tripped and hurt his ankle. I suppose Harry was trying to get away before he could be recognised."

"Harry Mersey? Good Lord! He wouldn't hurt Wesley. He must have been well and truly sloshed and fallen against him."

"The vicar said he pushed. The same as at the barbecue last year. He was drunk then, wasn't he?"

"We don't know that that was Harry. It could have been anyone."

"Well, it was him this time. He was coming round to borrow tools. He's told me several times that Wesley ought to be put away, but I didn't think he'd go to those lengths. I thought he just meant he should go into a Home."

"Of course he did. Harry's a really decent sort. But he does get sozzled. He couldn't have known what he was doing."

"The vicar must be going to see if he's sober enough to know it now, then," I suggested. "He said 'by arrangement' so he must have told Harry to go home and put his head under the tap or drink black coffee or whatever one does. Oh, poor Mary, when she learns about it!"

"She needn't be told. Mr. Jarrett can just give Harry a lecture on the evils of drink and tell him what he did when he gets him alone some time. I still find it almost impossible to believe that Harry would do a thing like that, however pickled he might be. But never mind that just now. I've a more important matter to discuss with you."

You can guess what that matter was. Every couple thinks it's something special with them at the time, but when you're as old as twenty-eight you're aware that countless people for countless years have felt the same way as you do. I guess we said much the same things, too. When the vicar returned we were engaged to be married.

He was walking with difficulty, clutching the doorway and the table for support. He flopped into a chair and we told him we were going to be married. "With you doing the job, please," added Julian.

"That will be my pleasure," said the vicar but he looked unhappy and worried.

"We've got it all worked out," I chattered on. "Julian's going to come to England to live. I'm sure he'll get a job and you're allowed to settle there if you marry a resident but we'll get married here first so his family can all be present and I'll have stayed my three months so it'll be the end of February, not too near

Easter when everyone else is getting married and that'll give Julian time to sell his share in the fish shop and . . . Mr. Jarrett, I don't believe you're listening."

He turned to me. "I beg your pardon, Pamela. I'm very pleased indeed that you and Julian intend to get married and I wish you every happiness. If I seemed distracted, it was not from any reservations I have on that score."

I guessed he'd had an unpleasant interview with Harry Mersey. I would have liked to know what had been said, but you don't ask a vicar things like that. Instead I asked, "How did you manage to drive, Mr. Jarrett?"

"With difficulty. I am not practised in using the same foot for clutch, accelerator and brake, and do not intend to risk the safety of the pedestrians in Auckland by doing it again if I can help it. Until my ankle recovers my curate will have to do all the visiting, and attend any meetings which are not in the church hall. Pamela, I forgot to give you back your suit jacket and your photograph. They're over there, on the top of the bookcase, see?"

I rose and got the jacket. "Thank you. I don't really want the photo of Talbot back."

"Who's Talbot?" asked Julian. "Do I have to be jealous?"

"No. He's just a man I knew in England. I've never mentioned him to you because he wasn't important enough to mention." I took up the photo. "Oh, it's still got some heroin on it, Mr. Jarrett. Is it all right to handle it?"

"Handle it as much as you like. I'm sorry I didn't wipe it properly for you. But the powder on it can do you no harm."

"But . . . heroin?"

"It's not heroin. I knew as much as soon as I first examined it. The colour, smell and texture are quite different. I was not sure what it was, however, so I had it analysed."

"But Mr. Bronson had it analysed and the police did, too. They said his sample was pure heroin."

"No doubt it was. But the powder on that photograph, and, I am sure, the powder in the pill box, were pure french chalk."

"I don't understand."

"Sit down, Pamela. First, I must apologise to you for speaking so sharply at the pool. *Anger resteth in the bosom of fools.*"

"I guess you had a right to be cross. I hadn't done as you told me to. But it was just not thinking. I wasn't deliberately ignoring what you'd said."

"I know that."

"You'd assured me my life was not in danger, so I didn't know why I mustn't trust Wesley and I wasn't afraid any more . . . though I still don't know why I was brought out here."

"You were never in danger of your life," said the vicar. "You were brought out for a special purpose—to play the rôle of murderer."

"What?" Julian and I both stared at him.

"I urged you not to be alone with

238

Wesley, but you misunderstood the reason for that. I could not tell you. I could not voice suspicions which I hoped were unfounded. You were not in danger, but Wesley was. I vented unwarranted anger on you because I was upset. It is not pleasant to have one's fears confirmed, or to look on the face of a man while he is in the act of attempting to drown his brother."

"Brother? You mean . . . Mr. Bronson?"

"Fortunately the girls told me you were left at the house with Wesley, but I was not unduly worried until they mentioned that they'd phoned their father to tell him you would deal with an expected caller. I then realised that it could be the opportunity Maxwell Bronson had been waiting for. I drove to the house as fast as I could and when I saw Bronson's car parked down the road, I ran. You know the rest. I was just in time to see Bronson in the act of pushing Wesley off the bench into the pool. He hoped he had not been recognised and tried to get away. If I had not arrived then Wesley would undoubt-edly have drowned, possibly by being held under the water. You, Pamela, were to be the scapegoat."

"Me? But I wasn't anywhere near him."

"It would have been self-defence on your part, not deliberate murder. Wesley had attacked you, you had struggled to free yourself, and by a most unfortunate accident, Wesley had fallen in the pool and drowned. Bronson would have test-ified on your behalf . . . other incidents had occurred . . . you were in no way to blame . . ."

"But I'd have denied the whole thing."

"You, a woman who had been found carrying a large amount of heroin? The quickest way to discredit anyone in this country is to have them found in possession of drugs. Your word against that of a well-known, respected company director. The powder was planted in your bag by Bronson to discredit you from the start. He had acquired a small amount of pure heroin which he would present to a chemist and the police. Of course, he had to wipe your bag out thoroughly and remove all traces of what was only french chalk."

"But why? Why did he want to kill Wesley? I know Wesley is a bit of a nuisance to him, but he's always spoken kindly of him."

"The words of his mouth were smoother than butter but war was in his heart. It was greed and resentment which drove him to it. The common situation of two brothers, one deprived of what he considered his rights."

"But that was Wesley. He was the one deprived. Mentally damaged, and knowing it. Not able to do what his brother could."

"Wesley has always accepted that fact, as most retarded persons do. Maxwell was the envious one, bitterly resentful that his father had changed his will and left the bulk of his estate to Wesley."

"But Mr. Bronson is wealthy, isn't he? He paid my fare out here."

"Riches make themselves wings. They

fly off as an eagle towards heaven. Not only had indignation at what Maxwell considered injustice been gnawing at him for years, but he began to have need of funds. He tells me that some of the businesses he controls are foundering, as so many are in these depressed times. A few hundred thousand, which he considered should rightly belong to him anyway, would have put them on their feet again. So he devised this plan. At the last moment he threw in another suspect —Harry Mersey—telling you he was coming to borrow tools. Mersey's hours of work are irregular, he is frequently under the influence of drink and he may not have been able to produce an alibi. You or Mersey—the police could have their choice."

"It seems an awfully complicated way to kill someone."

"Can you suggest a better? Certainly assassins can be hired, but how would a man in Bronson's position know of one? And what a risk to take!"

"An accident?"

"Would at once have put him under suspicion. Half a million or more dollars are involved. Premeditated murder is nearly always committed for monetary gain, and even if nothing could be proved, suspicion would remain. Also, there would be questioning, involvement with police, perhaps publicity. An accident would not be fool-proof. But his daughters suggested what to him, on further thought, appeared to be an excellent solution. An unknown woman from the other side of the world. He could not ask his agent for one of doubtful character or one with a police record, so he would have to cast doubt on her integrity after she arrived. He had a few weeks to get hold of a little heroin."

"No wonder he wiped out the bag so thoroughly."

"Yes, he invented a good reason for that. It was not until you told me that there had been a pill box full of powder that I doubted his story. He didn't know much about drugs, which is to his credit. His plan was to blacken your character,

Pamela, have you listed on police files as a suspected person and then suggest animosity towards you on Wesley's part by arranging a series of apparent attempts by Wesley to hurt or kill you. When the right opportunity came there would be one last such attack on you. You would defend yourself and Wesley would die."

"Did Fiona suspect?"

"I doubt it. Bronson is a good father and a considerate husband. But I wouldn't be surprised if his mother feared some plot on his part."

"She warned me," I told him. "She urged me to go home, just as you did, and she talked of the ill-feeling one brother could have against another. But I thought she was referring to Wesley."

"They were her sons. Parents are notoriously ignorant of their children's desires, fears, imaginings and secret activities. But no one, *no one* has a sounder knowledge of a man's moral character than his own mother. She knew one of her sons had a soul corroded with envy."

I looked down at the photograph I was holding. "If I hadn't kept Talbot, you might never have known the truth. Thank you, Talbot. I'm glad I didn't throw you into the harbour."

"Let me see the fellow," said Julian. "Hm, he's good-looking."

"I never want to see him again. He's served his purpose."

There was a brief silence and then I said, "How terrible it will be now for old Mrs. Bronson! And Fiona, with her husband in prison, and those poor girls. What will happen, Mr. Jarrett? Will you tell the police or have you persuaded him to give himself up?"

"Neither," said the vicar. "It is as well to consider carefully the results of any action before embarking on it. Let us do so in this case. Bronson could be committed for trial and with my testimony would probably be convicted of attempted murder and sent to prison. Five, ten years in the company of hardened criminals, junkies, pushers, thugs, child molesters. At his age of fifty-five, do you consider that experience would be remedial? Would it miraculously erase the black hate in his heart?

"What is the danger to others if he remains free? He will not dare another attempt on Wesley's life and his only grudge was against Wesley, through greed to obtain what he considered his rightful inheritance. He is not a murderer by nature. Consider the effects on his family if he is charged. What will be the emotional distress of the two girls when they learn their father is a potential killer?

"I have had a long talk with him and we have made certain plans. I shall tell no one, not even his wife, of the incident this morning. In return he will do as I suggest. Wesley will go into the Fairhaven Home. It is an exclusive establishment where he will have his own flat and he can take the dog with him. There is provision for meals in a common dining-room and a certain amount of mild supervision, but he can come and go as he pleases. He can take his stereo and indulge his hobbies. They have a well-equipped workshop. He will be as free as he is at the Bronsons' but there will always be someone to turn to if he needs help."

"Harry Mersey always said Wesley should be in a Home. I thought he was being nasty."

Julian spoke up. "Harry? Nasty? He's one of the best-hearted guys I know. A bit fond of the bottle but a thoroughly good chap. You'll get to know him better before we leave. I'll see to that."

The vicar continued, "Bronson is going to take his family, including his mother, to Norfolk Island for a week's holiday. He will try to arrange a booking for this Friday. That will avoid embarrassing association with his brother. By the time they return Wesley will be safely settled in Fairhaven. You, Pamela, will not stay in the house again until the Bronsons have left for Norfolk, then you can move back to your flat. Mr. Bronson does not know that you and Julian are aware of what happened, so there should be no embarrassment on his part when the family return and by then you will, I hope, have recovered from the shock and be able to behave normally in his presence. I doubt if you could do so now.

"I want you and Julian to go back to the house now, while the others are still out, and collect whatever clothes you will need for the next few days. You will stay with one of my parishioners until the Bronsons leave for Norfolk. Mrs. Hurley is a very pleasant, kind woman, whom I am sure you will like. She has recently been smitten with arthritis and will be glad of a little help in the house until her husband returns from a business trip on Saturday. I shall explain to Fiona Bronson that I have prevailed on you to stay with her."

He was dictating what I should do, as if from habit of taking command. But I didn't argue. It seemed a good idea. I asked, "What will you tell Wesley?"

Mr. Jarrett smiled. "Wesley takes life as it comes. Once again, someone has pushed him into the pool. These things happen. He wasn't so frightened this time, but he must be more careful in future. There's no swimming pool at Fairhaven, just shallow duck ponds which no one would want to push him into. What a nice place to go! I imagine that will be the tenor of his thoughts. He won't enquire who pushed him."

"Was it Mr. Bronson who pushed him in the pool at the barbecue last year? Was it an attempt to kill Wesley then and make it look like an accident?"

"I did not ask him and I do not intend to do so. The dim light and the crowds at the barbecue would certainly have offered a tempting opportunity."

"You're keeping all this from his family," I pointed out. "Yet you've told *us*. How do you know we won't talk about it? You said I was *without discretion*."

"I have not sworn you to secrecy. You are at liberty to tell anyone you like. But *whoso keepeth his mouth and his tongue keepeth his soul from trouble*. You are both intelligent, understanding persons

in whose judgment I have every confidence."

And that *was* a nice thing to have said
to one by someone as familiar with human
frailty as the vicar of St. Bernard's!

16

JULIAN bought me a ring next day and when we knew Mr. Bronson would be at work we went to tell the rest of the family our news. Fiona seemed genuinely pleased, especially as a new future would be opening up for Julian. "He has incentive now," she remarked. "He'll get a job in England where he can make better use of his qualifications. There'll be no more fish and chip shops." I wasn't so sure myself but I didn't comment. Whatever Julian chose to do would be all right with me.

The girls were disappointed that their favourite uncle would be going away but we told them we expected them over for a holiday as soon as Diella had finished secondary school. Charis would have had a year at University then, so they could both come over before the new term

251

started in March. And they must both be bridesmaids at the wedding.

"So *that's* why you're not coming to Norfolk with us," said Charis. "I thought Dad was a bit mean not taking you, too."

"I didn't want to come," I assured her. "Julian and I have so much to discuss and the wedding to plan. I'm going to ask your uncle Harry to give me away."

"Oh, neat!"

The aunts reacted much the same way as Fiona. It was hard to tell what Wesley thought about it. He was happy at the prospect of moving to Fairhaven, far happier than we'd expected him to be. Julian thought that was because he would no longer feel a burden or a nuisance to his brother and his family. But one never knew what was going on in Wesley's mind. His flat there was ready for him and we helped him shift in on Thursday, the day before the family left for Norfolk Island.

It was pleasant staying with Mrs. Hurley, who is a perfect dear, but I visited the Bronsons each day. Mr.

Bronson happened to be home on one occasion. He congratulated us and wished us happiness but he looked far from happy himself. His face was drawn and pasty and I couldn't help feeling a little sorry for him. To have an attempted murder on your conscience for the rest of your life must be no light burden.

On Saturday I moved back to the now empty Bronson house. Fiona had left a pile of groceries and fruit for me and her library card to use if I wished. For two days I enjoyed a lazy life, reading, sun-bathing, swimming in the pool and enjoying the few visits that Julian had time to make. All the time, however, something kept niggling at the back of my mind—that horrible Mr. Smith, the lie he had told about his blond friend and what he'd said about snoopers. I wished I'd told the vicar all about it. The other events had pushed it into the background for a day or two, but I should have gone to see him by now and asked his advice. I wouldn't bother him in the weekend, because he'd be so busy then, and

Monday was his day off. It would be mean to break into that. I'd definitely phone him up on Tuesday, though. I didn't go to church on the Sunday—the sun and the pool were too tempting and I felt no obligation to go now the girls weren't there. But he wouldn't mind that. He'd let me talk and probably assure me there was nothing to worry about. Of course, there *was* nothing to worry about. The Smith man had promised he wouldn't contact me again, and he had no need to say that unless he meant it. But I remained uneasy. I'd been stupid not to tell the whole story earlier to both Julian and the vicar.

"You're a fool," said the clock in the hall. "Fool, ger-FOOL, pause . . . fool, ger-FOOL, pause . . ."

Then this morning . . . how long ago was it? An hour? Two hours? Someone knocked at the back door of my flat. I opened it and saw a big burly chap in a sports coat and checked shirt, carrying some blue and green striped teatowels over his arm.

"Am I speaking to Miss Pamela Martin?"

"Yes, that's me."

Then it happened. All so suddenly and unexpectedly that I couldn't do a thing about it. He strode in, shut the door and pulled my arms behind my back. I yelled and tried to kick but he took no notice. Before I could put up a decent fight my hands were tied with one of those teatowels, I was pushed down onto a kitchen chair and my legs were tied, too. That may sound as if I'm a puny weakling. I'm not. But it was all so quick my reactions were slow. He didn't have a gun. He didn't have a knife. But he had experience, you could tell that.

"What are you doing? What do you want? My purse is in the other room. I'll get you all the money I have."

"Don't want your money, lady."

"Well, if you're going to ransack the house, there's no need to tie me up. I couldn't stop you."

"Not after your silver. Just carrying out orders." He had started to readjust the teatowels he'd bound me with. He undid and re-tied the one round my wrists, then he tied each of my ankles separately to a chair leg.

"Not so tight. That hurts." Women in novels wriggled their hands until they worked them free. But it seems he'd read those novels, too.

"Gotta be tight. But no bruises. Mustn't leave bruises. That'll do ya." Then he pulled out a cord from his pocket—it looked like a nylon fishing line —and proceeded to tie the chair to the kitchen table and then run a length of cord round the heavy refrigerator and the table leg nearest it. I was dragged along on my chair as he pulled the table towards the refrigerator.

"What are you going to do to me?"

He regarded me with the cold, dispassionate look I have seen men bestow on a flapping fish they have just landed on the wharf, the uninterested, uncaring glance as they toss it behind them, without even considering the common decency of a coup de grâce.

"I'm not the hit man, sister," he told me. "I'm not going to do anything to you. Not my job. His. I just gotta make sure you're here when he comes."

"What will the . . . the hit man do?"

He considered this question with some mild interest. "Don't rightly know in this case. It's not as though you double-crossed anyone. You just know too much. A shot of the pure uncut'd be my guess. Quick and painless."

"You don't look unkind," I said. What a lie! He looked as if he'd had a lifetime of violence and hate boiling in his soul. "Won't you please let me go?"

"More than my life's worth," he told me. "I got nothing against you personally, but it's you or me. The boss don't take kindly to not having his orders carried out. Gotta gag you, too," he added chattily.

"No one can hear me from here."

"Orders. Gotta gag you. But no bruises. I guess he wants to leave the syringe and make it look like you did it yourself." He was checking the knots of the cords round the table. I must talk to him while I could. How to persuade him? Soften him? No, not a hope. Threaten him? Frighten him? I must appear to be unworried, confident.

"You won't get away with it," I said, trying to control the tremor in my voice.

He didn't bother to answer and I could hardly blame him. It was a silly, trite phrase, a television cliché. Be more specific. "I'm expecting someone soon."

"Like hell you are."

"I certainly am. He'll be here shortly."

"Don't be a fool. You're not expecting anyone. Cut out the bluff. It don't work." He was testing the cloths round my ankles and decided to add another teatowel. I had very little time. Talk, I must talk while I could. Use speech, the only thing left to me. After all, I'd been brought over here because of my speech. Let it work in my own interests now. Oh God, let it work! I looked at his ruthless face and had an idea. I might be able to use the very fact that he had no vestige of sympathy. If I was right . . . but it wouldn't work if he had a heart.

"It's no bluff," I said and tried to give a carefree laugh. It sounded like a spoon scraping the bottom of a saucepan. "The vicar of St. Bernard's is coming round. Mr. Jarrett. He'll be here soon. I have to tell him which of two hymns I've chosen for my wedding. I promised to make up my mind by this morning and he's calling in on his way to a luncheon to find out which it is."

"There'll be no wedding for you, lady. Your friends'll be singing the hymns."

"All right, *don't* believe me. I'm not worried. Mr. Jarrett, the vicar of St. Bernard's is coming to get the number of the hymn and he'll untie me." Again I attempted what was meant to sound like an unconcerned chuckle. I must babble now. "We're getting married in a fortnight, you see, and he wants to know the hymn so he can tell the organist and he said he'd drop in this morning just before lunch, so my fiancé and I had to choose yesterday. You see, we just hadn't been

259

able to make up our minds whether to have number 157 or 300, they're both suitable, and we chose 300 because it . . . oh! I mean we couldn't decide . . . we have to look . . ." I let my voice falter off as if conscious of the blue I'd made.

"*What* number?"

"I don't know which one yet. I didn't choose. We couldn't decide. We'll talk about it when the vicar comes. Yes, that's it. Mr. Jarrett's coming to help me choose which one to have."

For the first time a small doubt showed in his green piggy eyes. He'd heard all right. "300, eh? Well, I guess the vicar can be informed. Save him the trouble of coming."

"Oh, please, don't do that," I begged him. "He won't come if you do that. Oh, have a heart. You can say you tied me up. It won't be your fault if Mr. Jarrett finds me before your . . . your hit man comes. He can't take it out on you because you've carried out your orders. Oh, please, *please!* I'm not asking you to let me go. I know you can't do that. But just let Mr. Jarrett come. Don't stop him, that's all, I ask. Just don't phone him . . ." I burst into tears. No effort, no acting. It was part of my plan but I was frightened to sobs and they came unbidden. I was still blubbering as he took a teatowel, stuffed a portion of it into my mouth and secured it by means of another teatowel round my head.

"Don't you worry, lady. Hymn 300, eh? I'll see he gets the message. Save the poor fellow a trip. There, that'll keep you quiet, won't it?"

I didn't answer. You can't when your mouth is stuffed with teatowel. He didn't even look at me as he left the house. It wasn't sympathy that kept him from doing so. It was just lack of interest. He'd done his job, he'd carried out his orders. The hit man would take over from here and the boss would be satisfied. What was the "pure uncut"? Heroin, I supposed. If it was going to look like suicide they'd have to make jabs all over me to suggest I was an addict. It would be merciful to give me the big dose first.

I did not hear him leave the property. He must have gone, as he came, with a silent tread. Since then I've been waiting, hoping . . . despairing. Would he really phone the vicar? It would be prudent to do so as a precaution even if he didn't fully believe me. I'd given him the name of the church twice and the name of the vicar several times and they were both listed in the phone book. A matter-of-fact, polite message, he might reason, would be all the vicar wanted. Miss Martin had asked him to let the vicar know that the hymn she had chosen was 300. Oh, if he only would! Before the other—the hit man—comes. If he has any sense he *will* ring the vicar. But suppose the vicar's not home? He should be. It's Monday, his day off, so he won't have any services and meetings and he won't be visiting his family because his ankle's still too bad to drive with, Julian said. Though in a real emergency he'd drive. Like now, if that man phones him. But he *could* be out . . . oh, I don't know. I'm too confused. I can't think straight. I hope the hit man makes a quick job of it. Quick and painless, he said . . . no, the vicar won't come because the man won't phone. Or he'll come too late. Even if he comes, the hit man will get here first. Or will he? I can't do a thing. I can't wriggle my wrists. I can't even move them. I can't shift the chair, I can't bump it loudly enough for any neighbour to hear. There's no chance whatever of getting free. I can hear the traffic out in the road. And I can hear that detestable clock in the hall, sneering, gloating. You're going to die, ger-DIE, pause . . . die, ger-DIE, pause . . . die, ger-DIE. . .

I'll never see my darling Julian again. I hope he doesn't care too much when they find my body. I must be calm. Face the hit man with dignity. Go out with grace . . . Though the vicar *might* come . . . *if* he was phoned . . . if he was home . . . there's just a chance . . . oh, I don't know. I can't think, I can't remember, I can't reason. My mind's just a whirling jelly.

A car's stopping outside on the road.

The gate's opening . . . someone's coming in. This is *it!* The hit man or the vicar? I can hear footsteps now . . . they're coming round the side of the house . . . halting footsteps, uneven like the menacing throb of that horrible clock in the hall. Clip, ger-CLOP, pause . . . clip, ger-CLOP, pause . . . clip, ger-CLOP. . . They've stopped. He's at the door . . . A knock . . . Now the handle's turning. *Oh my God, which one will it be?*

Other titles in the
Linford Mystery Library:

A GENTEEL LITTLE MURDER
by Philip Daniels

Gilbert had a long-cherished plan to murder his wife. When the polished Edward entered the scene Gilbert's attitude was suddenly changed.

DEATH AT THE WEDDING
by Madelaine Duke

Dr. Norah North's search for a killer takes her from a wedding to a private hospital. She deals with the nastiest kind of criminal—the blackmailer and rapist!

MURDER FIRST CLASS
by Ron Ellis

A new type of criminal announces his intention of personally restoring the death penalty in England. Will Detective Chief Inspector Glass find the Post Office robbers before the Executioner gets to them?

THE DRACULA MURDERS
by Philip Daniels

The Horror Ball was interrupted by a spectral figure who warned the merrymakers they were tampering with the unknown. Then a girl was ritualistically murdered on the golf course.

THE LADIES OF LAMBTON GREEN
by Liza Shepherd

Why did murdered Robin Colquhoun's picture pose such a threat to the ladies of Lambton Green?

CARNABY AND THE GAOLBREAKERS
by Peter N. Walker

Detective Sergeant James Aloysius Carnaby-King is sent to prison as bait. When he joins in an escape he is thrown headfirst into a vicious murder hunt.

VICIOUS CIRCLE
by Alan Evans

Crawford finds himself on the run and hunted in a strange land, wanting only to find his son but prepared to pay any cost.